PRAISE FOR GAIL GAYMER MARTIN:

"Gail Gaymer Martin's best book to date.
Real conflict and very likeable characters
enhance this wonderful romantic story."
—*Romantic Times* on *Loving Hearts*

"Perhaps Gail Gaymer Martin's best,
a romantic suspense novel you'll want to read—
during the day!"
—*Romantic Times* on *A Love for Safekeeping*

"…an emotional, skillfully written story
about mature subject matter. You'll probably
need a box of tissues for this one."
—*Romantic Times* on *Upon a Midnight Clear*

❧ ❧ ❧

PRAISE FOR CYNTHIA RUTLEDGE:

"Cynthia Rutledge jumps off the beaten track
again, with another notable book."
—*Romantic Times* on *Wedding Bell Blues*

"Characterizations and voice
are her usual high standard."
—*Romantic Times* on *Judging Sara*

"There is nothing typical about this
wonderful story. *The Marrying Kind*
is another winner from start to finish!"
—*Romantic Times* on *The Marrying Kind*

GAIL GAYMER MARTIN

lives with her real-life hero in Lathrup Village, Michigan. Growing up in nearby Madison Heights, Gail wrote poems and stories as a child and progressed to writing professional journals, skits and poems for teachers, and programs for her church. When she retired, she tried her hand at her dream—writing novels.

Gail is a multipublished author in nonfiction and fiction with ten novels and five novellas, and many more to come. Her Steeple Hill Love Inspired romances *Upon a Midnight Clear* and *Loving Treasures* won Holt Medallions in 2001 and 2003. Besides writing, Gail enjoys singing, public speaking and presenting writers' workshops. She believes that God's gift of humor gets her through even the darkest moments and praises God for His blessings. Visit her Web site at www.gailmartin.com. She loves to hear from her readers. E-mail her at gail@gailmartin.com or write to P.O. Box 760063, Lathrup Village, MI 48076.

CYNTHIA RUTLEDGE

grew up wanting to write books. She wrote her first book at fourteen, but when it received less than stellar reviews from those she let read it, she relegated it to the trash and didn't write again for years. She started writing again as an adult and sold her first book to Steeple Hill in 1999. That book, *Unforgettable Faith,* will always be special to her because it opened the door to her career at Steeple Hill. It remains the only book set in her home state of Nebraska.

"Loving Grace" is Cynthia's eighth title for Love Inspired. Her July 2002 Love Inspired novel, *Wedding Bell Blues,* was nominated for a Bookseller's Best Award. She has also written two books for Silhouette Romance.

THE HARVEST

GAIL GAYMER MARTIN
CYNTHIA RUTLEDGE

Love Inspired.

Published by Steeple Hill Books

STEEPLE HILL BOOKS

Steeple
Hill®

ISBN 0-373-87230-5

THE HARVEST

Copyright © 2003 by Steeple Hill Books, Fribourg, Switzerland

ALL GOOD GIFTS
Copyright © 2003 by Gail Gaymer Martin

LOVING GRACE
Copyright © 2003 by Cynthia Rutledge

Visit us at www.steeplehill.com

Printed in U.S.A.

CONTENTS

Dear Reader,

I'm excited to share this book with my friend Cynthia Rutledge. Writing stories set around Thanksgiving brings warm memories of families and friends, and reminds us of God's goodness. It's a time to thank and praise the Lord for all of His blessings. One blessing that stands out in my mind is my parents' lakefront property outside Mackinaw City, with its magnificent view of the Mackinac Bridge spanning the Straits for five miles, and the sight of quaint Mackinac Island. This locale—the quiet woods, rolling waves and night sky with a million stars—is the major setting for "All Good Gifts." I always feel so close to God in the hush of the Mackinaw woods. May the Lord bless you always as you offer your thanksgiving.

"Loving Grace" brings back Nick Tucci, a man we first met in the book *Judging Sara*. The main character in that book was Nick's brother "Crow," whom we'd first met in *Undercover Angel*. Sounds kind of like a soap opera, doesn't it? Actually you can blame this all on my childhood. When I was a young girl, I loved books with recurring characters, and that's why you often see them in my stories. I hope you enjoy reading "Loving Grace" and Gail Gaymer Martin's "All Good Gifts," and that your upcoming holiday season is filled with God's blessings.

Gail Gaymer Martin

Cynthia Rutledge

ALL GOOD GIFTS

Gail Gaymer Martin

* * *

In memory of my mother,
who loved our Mackinaw property
and whose artwork helps it live on.
—GGM

For everything God created is good,
and nothing is to be rejected if it is received
with thanksgiving, because it is consecrated
by the word of God and prayer.

—*1 Timothy* 4:4-5

Chapter One

Thump. Thump.

Tess Britton lowered the poker and listened while her free hand pressed against her heart. Was that the sound of her own throbbing pulse or something else…something outside?

She listened again.

Thump.

A shiver coursed through her. She moved to the front window and looked toward the sloped path heading to the lake. Surrounded by pine trees and a shrouded moon, Tess saw only blackness.

She shook her head at her nervous reaction and drew her shoulders upward in a calming breath. How foolish. The cabin had always served as a getaway— her sanctuary—but in the evening, the quiet, natural setting set her on edge. Even when Al had been at her side, the rustle and skitter coming from outside sent her nerves vacillating like a yo-yo.

Since she'd been widowed, her life had changed in far more ways than just experiencing jitters in the dark. She felt abandoned, deceived by Al…and by God. Her dreams and hopes had faded away like tonight's cloud-covered moon, leaving her shrouded in unanswered questions and self-created answers that caused her guilt and fear.

Tess lifted her gaze to the sky and thought of God. How long had it been since she'd prayed? Forever, it seemed. Though black and silent, the heavens glimmered with pinpricks of stars. One glowing orb stood out among the rest, its beams stretching and glinting into the blackness. A silent hope…a prayer lifted heavenward. A prayer that something would shine in her life again.

Tess pushed herself away from the window, feeling like a child wishing on a star. Wishes and dreams had no connection with the real world. She'd gotten over Al's death, but not the circumstances. Not the horrible reality she learned that day. Could she ever trust a man again?

Shaking her head, she returned to the fireplace and took a couple of prodding pokes, hoping to dispel the dank gloom that surrounded her. She'd arrived in Mackinaw City at dusk and drove to the property in the woods along the shore. When she arrived, Tess had walked into the damp, cold cabin, shaking from the October chill.

Now the warmth from the fireplace helped. When she turned away, instead of returning to her chair and her half-read novel, Tess headed toward the kitchen-ell off the living room. She snapped on the radio, rotating the dial and settling on the only station she could find, a combination of country music and static. She crossed to the stove and turned on the burner under the teakettle. A warm drink would feel comforting on a chilly evening.

Tess searched through the carton she'd carried in earlier and found the cocoa mix, then grabbed a cup and spoon. As she dipped into the mixture, another ponderous thud sent her heart pumping while cocoa dust splayed across the counter and onto the floor.

"Calm down," she said aloud, pausing a moment to settle her nerves.

She cleaned up the mess, then blew a puff of pent-up air from her cheeks as she went and plopped into her chair and flipped open her novel. The tension that crept up the back of her neck to her temples was becoming a throbbing headache. While Tess forced her eyes to focus on the book, she kept half an eye on the clock and half an ear on the teakettle.

She waited and listened.

The words blurred, and aroused by the silence, she checked the clock, then the stove.

No steam. No whistle. Nothing.

She rose and touched the kettle. Lukewarm. Her spirits sank.

The propane.

Feeling self-pity, Tess bit her lower lip. She'd watched both Al and her brother switch the tanks, but she'd never paid much attention. Now she prayed she'd remember what they'd done. Someday she'd pay for a gas line.

Someday? Maybe not. A new thought had entered her mind on the three-hundred-mile trip up north. She should sell the cabin. Not that she wanted to. It just made sense. The possibility crushed her heart like a steamroller.

Facing her newest task, Tess slipped on her jacket, then grabbed the red toolbox from a storage cupboard and a flashlight to guide her. She hated feeling inept. All her life she'd been self-assured and confident...until Al's death. Now she questioned everything. Her ability. Her wisdom. Her judgment.

Outside, the cold breeze rattled the dried leaves that crunched underfoot as she marched with fabricated confidence to the back of the cabin.

She set the toolbox on the ground, opened it and found a wrench. But when she straightened, another sound rustled in the underbrush.

Holding her breath, she paused and listened.

Porcupine? Skunk?

Too ponderous.

A bear?

The thought quivered through her limbs. She'd heard about bears in the area.

She swung the beam into the woods, then thought better and snapped off the light as she pressed her back against the cabin and peered into the inky night.

The cabin's cedar shakes sent a damp chill up her spine, but she clung to the wall and gaped at a hulking shape emerging from the trees. She swallowed the gasp that struggled to escape.

The strapping silhouette lumbered in her direction. Her fingers trembled against the flashlight while she gripped the wrench in the other hand, wondering how much damage the implement could do to a hungry bear.

The form drew nearer. Leaves shifted and crunched beneath its lumbering steps. Her pulse hammered in her ears.

It came closer.

Her legs trembled and her prayer flew to heaven as a solution shot into her thoughts. Animals feared light. Grasping her only hope, she raised the flashlight to brandish the beam.

Instead, the dark form clasped her arm like a vise.

Tess's scream pierced the night sky, accompanied by a deep baritone bellow. Her knees buckled, and an arm caught her as the flashlight and wrench tumbled to the ground.

"What are you doing?" the voice demanded.

Tess jerked away from the stranger's clutches. She reeled backward, bracing herself against the cabin. "What are *you* doing? This is private property."

"Yes, I know. Who are you?" A light snapped on and aimed a precision shaft into Tess's eyes, blinding her from the towering figure.

She threw her hand across her face to block the glare. "I'm the owner." She masked her fear, spitting out her words with as much indignation as she could muster.

When she bent to retrieve her flashlight, a wave of nausea rolled through her, and she crouched, afraid to rise.

The light followed her downward motion. "Sorry." His gruff voice softened. "Are you okay?"

"I'm fine," Tess said, swallowing the bile that crept up her throat. She rose, her own light now aimed into the face of the fearful hulk. Her pulse beat in double time as she looked into vaguely familiar eyes.

His curiosity faded to concern. "I'm really sorry. Are you sure you're okay?"

"I'm fine except you scared the life out of me. What are you doing skulking through the woods this time of night?"

He gestured toward the lake. "I like to walk on the beach at night. No law against that, is there?" An amused expression flickered on his face.

"No…but there is against scaring someone to death."

"I didn't mean to do that. I saw the light beam coming from behind the cabin and I veered through the woods—" he gave her a telling look "—to startle the burglar. They've had some break-ins nearby."

The news flash darted through her already-jittered senses. "Thanks for the wonderful bit of information."

The man's expression shifted to earnestness. "Sorry, but you should know. The cabin on the other side of my sister's was robbed."

Her annoyance faded as his undertaking clarified

in her mind. How could she be angry at someone who'd endangered himself to protect her property. "Thanks. I'm sorry for being so unpleasant."

His tone lightened. "I scared you. You're forgiven."

The rest of his comment awoke in Tess's thoughts. "What do you mean, your sister? Who is she?"

"Jill Roddy. Two cottages down. Short, blond—"

"Jill? Sure. We've talked on the beach many times. And I love her little boy, Davie."

"My nephew." He nodded as if agreeing. "You and I have met before. I don't suppose you remember." He shifted the flashlight to the left hand and extended his right. "I'm Ryan Walsh."

"Ryan?" She accepted his handshake, allowing her memory to take her back to many sun-filled afternoons. "Yes, I remember. I'm Tess Britton." She searched his face, recalling the vague familiarity but wondering about the change. "But you look so different."

"I had a beard then. Plus a few extra pounds."

"Is that it?" His amiable smile sent warmth humming along Tess's limbs. "Your face struck a chord when I first saw you." His eyes, she corrected herself.

For a moment they stood with clasped hands while they studied each other in the light beam.

Recalling their earlier meetings, Tess's gaze went on an admiring new journey over his tall build and broad shoulders. She returned her focus to his perfect features—the chiseled jaw, a generous smile, a shock of unruly blond hair and green eyes that were like new grass sparkling with dew.

"Are you alone on this trip?" he asked.

She lowered her eyes, not wanting to ruin the moment with explanation. "Yes."

"I suppose your husband had to work again. That's too bad."

Work again. His statement surprised her while an awkward silence stretched between them. Apparently, he'd remembered how often she'd come up north alone or with her brother and his wife.

Ryan looked at her a moment, then took a step backward. "Did I say something wrong?"

"No. My husband died two years ago."

"I—I'm sorry." He shifted his feet and lowered his head. "My big mouth."

Her gaze settled on his well-formed lips, looking soft and tempting in the moonlight. She winced seeing how uncomfortable he appeared. "Please...you didn't know. I'm fine now, really." For the most part, she added to herself.

"That's me. Open mouth. Insert foot."

"Please. Forget it."

Another suffocating silence wavered between them. Finally, Tess broke the stillness.

"Well, now," she said, hoping to lighten the mood, "I suppose we look pretty silly standing in the dark introducing ourselves."

Ryan turned his head one way, then the other, peering into the blackness. "Could be, but I don't see anyone watching us." He shot her a tender smile.

Her pulse fluttered with his gentle humor. "Guess not." Then remembering her purpose, Tess swung her light toward the propane tanks. "I'd better finish this job."

Ryan's gaze followed the direction of the beam. "Propane?"

"Uh-huh. The tank ran out, but the other's full...I hope."

He crouched to check the gauge, and his action scented the air with a mixture of new leather and a woodsy fragrance.

Patting the tank, he rose. "You're right. This one's full. Let me give you a hand."

Tess wanted to say she could do it herself, but she hesitated...wondering if she really could.

He shone the flashlight downward and picked up the wrench from where she'd dropped it.

Eager to accept his offer, Tess directed her light as he made quick work of rotating the tanks.

"There you go." He straightened and handed Tess the wrench, his eyes focused on hers.

His direct gaze took her breath away.

As she mumbled her thanks, her thoughts drifted to the long lonely evening and to the present amiable company. "Would you like to come in for some cocoa?"

"Cocoa?" His eyebrows flickered above his smiling eyes. "Sure. Sounds good."

The tension vanished.

Tess released a tethered breath and aimed the light

to guide her steps around the cabin. Ryan followed, and she stepped aside for him to enter first.

Inside, the warmth of the fireplace greeted them, and the static had vanished from the radio station. The air hummed with a soft tune.

Tess slid off her jacket and reached for his. Beneath it, Ryan wore a rust-colored crewneck that stretched across his expansive chest—the kind of chest she'd love to rest her head on.

Ryan paused near the door. His gaze swept the room before he crossed to the fireplace and lifted his palms to the warmth. "Nice place. Heat feels good."

"A bit rustic, but thanks," Tess said, hanging their jackets on a hook behind the door. "Have a seat, and I'll heat the water. Again." She sent him a grin, amazed that only minutes ago she'd felt so alone.

He sank into an overstuffed chair near the hearth, and Tess went and lit the pilot light, then turned on the burner. While she prepared the snack, her attention drifted across the great room to Ryan. He stared into the fire, his elbows resting on his knees. His thick, golden hair curved around his ears, and a lone lock curled on his forehead.

An unsettling feeling caught in her chest. Since Al's death, Tess hadn't looked at a man as anything but a member of the opposite sex. Today she looked at him as a *man,* an attractive available man whose image sent alien sensations coursing through her.

As if he knew she watched him, he glanced over his shoulder. She turned away, and when the kettle whistled, Tess made the cocoa and carried a tray to a table near the hearth.

Ryan admired the pretty woman handing him the steaming drink. The rich chocolate aroma rose from the thick mug, but another fragrance touched his senses as she leaned toward him. Lilies maybe. Ryan wasn't sure. He didn't know much about flowers, but he knew this—Tess Britton was as lovely as any blossom.

Outside, he'd been struck by her long, dark hair disheveled by the wind, fringing her fair face. And her eyes were the deepest blue he'd ever seen. When they'd met times earlier, he'd contained his attraction, remembering she was married. Now things were different. His gaze drifted heavenward, amazed at God's way of directing His children.

Tess settled in an easy chair across from him and stared into the fire. She leaned against the cushion, stretching her slender legs toward the flames. He remembered admiring her figure on the beach a couple years earlier, but most of all he remembered her smile and the way she played with his young nephew. He wondered why she didn't have a child of her own…but now wasn't the time to ask.

He'd made a blunder mentioning her husband, and he had cringed seeing the look on Tess's face. Their amiable mood had vanished as quickly as a rock pitched into Lake Huron. Ryan recalled Tess mentioning that her husband often worked weekends. He could barely remember the man.

He eyed her now, sitting across from him. He

wondered about her husband's death, but having occasional good sense, he harnessed that question, too.

When Tess turned away from the fireplace, she shifted her legs and curled them beneath her on the cushion before catching his gaze.

Ryan lifted the mug as if proposing a toast. "Tastes great. Takes off the chill."

She motioned toward the cheese plate. "I didn't bring much with me, but it's better than nothing, I suppose."

Beneath her geniality Ryan noted a tinge of discomfort...and why not? He'd been a virtual stranger who'd plodded out of the woods. He should be grateful she hadn't whacked him with the wrench.

The silence stretched until he reached over and cut a hunk from the cheddar block and grasped a few crackers.

She curved her hands around the ceramic mug. "You'll laugh if I tell you this."

He arched an eyebrow and waited.

"I thought you were a bear." An embarrassed grin curved the edge of her mouth.

"A bear?"

"When I saw your shadow, the shape looked hulking...until I realized it was you."

"Thanks...I think." Ryan liked the way her lips parted when she smiled and the way her cheeks dimpled.

She settled against the cushion, her attention drawn to the firelight. Ryan wrapped himself in the pleasant mood. Too much time had passed sense he'd felt this contented with a woman.

A comfortable silence settled over the room. Tess uncurled her legs and slid her hands along their shapely length to tug at her stockings, then regarded him with curious eyes. "Jill has only one brother, right?"

"You're looking at him."

He watched her expression change to a questioning frown. "Then you must be the brother who's getting married."

Chapter Two

Ryan's stomach knotted. How had she heard about Donna? His sister, naturally. He struggled with his response. He liked this woman and didn't want to create a bad impression. "When did Jill tell you I was getting married?"

"Early this summer. She mentioned Davie's going to be the ring bearer."

"Aah," he said, planting on a lighthearted smile and scuffling for time to think. Should he tell her his fiancée dumped him only a couple of weeks earlier? No. She'd think he was on the rebound. The cause for the breakup needed more explanation than he wanted to give so Ryan only offered a vague response. "We called the wedding off...a while ago."

"Oh. I'm sorry. Jill didn't mention it." She covered her lips with her fingers. "I guess it's my turn to withdraw my foot from my mouth."

"Not a problem." An unexpected sensation

wound through him, as if he wanted to take time now to tell her what happened. Someone else's perspective might help him dispel the guilt he felt over the situation. "We both realized it was a mistake."

"It's easier that way." She directed her gaze toward the fire. "Still, I'm sure it was difficult."

"Facing the truth is always difficult," Ryan said, noting a depth of meaning in her eyes. Having second thoughts, Ryan plowed through his mind for a new topic—anything to avoid talking about his situation. "Do you really remember when we met?"

Tess inched her head upward. "I sure do."

Ryan remembered the day well. She'd been alone, sitting on a canvas chair holding a book—a romance if he remembered correctly. When he and his nephew neared her, a flurry of seagulls had fluttered and squawked into the sky, and Tess had turned her head toward him and Davie. Her eyes had intrigued him even then.

"You were with Davie and the golden retriever," she said.

Ryan had forgotten about Buck.

"Your nephew is the sweetest boy. Behaves like an angel."

"Thanks. He is a good kid."

Her gaze lingered on his as she swept her fingers across her chin. "I didn't recognize you without the beard. You look good…both ways."

He thanked her, wishing she'd used some other adjective, like *handsome, debonair, good-looking.* Uneasy with his foolish thoughts, he refocused on

Tess and saw a look of longing in her eyes. "You like kids?"

"I always hoped I'd have a little boy—or girl— like Davie," she said.

Her expression tugged at his heartstrings. "Why didn't you?" The question sailed out before he could stop it. Way too personal.

She didn't answer at first, and Ryan could see her struggling with a response.

"We were waiting," she said finally, her voice so soft he almost didn't hear her.

Sadness hit him in the gut while she looked at him with regret-filled eyes and ran her hand along her neck. Ryan remained silent, wondering if she would say more.

She didn't, and feeling uneasy, Ryan searched for a response. "We all do that," he said finally. "Put things off. Then sometimes it's…too late." The truth struck him.

Tess's sudden melancholy permeated the air. Ryan sensed it was something deeper than wanting a child. He longed to sit beside her and put his arm around her shoulder to offer her comfort.

Why had she and her husband waited to have kids and why had her husband died? Questions tumbled in his thoughts until he stifled his curiosity and broke the silence. "We don't always understand why things happen." He said the words as much for himself as for her.

"I wanted kids, but Al…" The words sounded private as if they were meant only for her ears.

Tess didn't finish the thought. Instead, she shifted in the chair and sent him a sudden smile. "You don't want to listen to my rambling." She took a sip of the cocoa.

"I— We all need to get things off our chest." He thought of his own situation.

The room hummed with silence unil Tess rose and headed toward the fireplace. "You really like kids. I could tell that day on the beach." She grasped the poker and gave the glowing logs a jab.

Watching the firefly sparks, Ryan joined her. "You're right. I love 'em. I envy my sister." He took the poker from Tess's hand and prodded at the log as if he could jab away his thoughts. But her nearness nudged his spirit, and he decided to be open with her.

"That was one of the things that ended my engagement. Donna didn't want kids right away." Maybe never, he thought. "I figured I'm thirty-three, and I wanted to have children while I was young enough to enjoy them."

"Sounds familiar" was all Tess said.

Ryan replaced the poker in the stand and bent down to grasp a large log. He tossed it onto the flames. The sparks flew like red fireworks and the pungent scent filled the air.

Tess stood beside him a moment, then ambled toward the kitchen-ell as she spoke. "I could see how much you love Davie. That's what sticks in my mind."

"Someday, I'd like two or three just like him,"

Ryan said. Relishing the company and fire's warmth, he watched Tess putter at the stove.

"Me, too. Just the same." Then a tiny grin pulled at her mouth. "Maybe four."

"Four isn't bad," he agreed, sinking back into his seat.

They laughed, and it felt good. Natural and honest. He snatched up a cookie and took a bite. "Pretty good."

"Thanks," she said offhandedly as she returned with a carafe of hot cocoa and refilled their cups. "They're store-bought," she added, setting the container on the table. She curled up in the chair, looking small and vulnerable.

"What brought you up north this weekend?" he asked.

"I decided to spend a few days here, then close the cabin. My brother's been coming along to help since Al died, but this year he has his computer business, and… Well, I just couldn't ask him. Don't know what I'd do without my family."

"Me, neither. Jill listens to me more than anyone. I'd be lost without her two-cent opinions." He chuckled. "And her five bucks' worth of wisdom."

"Wisdom's nice."

Her comment had a double meaning, he guessed, but he had no idea what was needling her. "Since your brother couldn't make it," Ryan added, "I'll be happy to give you a hand."

"No, you've helped enough. I have to learn to do things on my own. But thanks."

"Let me teach you."

"Are you on vacation?" She rolled her eyes. "You must be desperate for things to do."

"No, I'm doing the 'brother' thing. I'm closing Jill's place for the season. Gary's in the hospital."

"Gary?" Her grin faded. "Nothing serious, I hope."

"Not really. Appendicitis. Who ever heard of an adult with appendicitis?"

"It happens."

"I figured I'd stay a few days and relax before going back. I have another reason for coming north, too. I'm doing a general appraisal on a house on Mackinac Island."

She leaned back and grasped her drink. "Appraisal? You're in real estate?" Her eyebrows rose as she looked at him over the mug's rim.

"Yes. And investments."

"I suppose that's good money."

"Not bad. But it's not so much the money."

Tess leaned forward and rested her elbows on her knees, her fingers wrapped around the mug. "Now you've really captured my interest."

He chuckled. "I'm a legal Peeping Tom. I step into people's private worlds and see how they live. It's intriguing." But not nearly as intriguing as you, Tess, he thought.

"Nothing wrong with that," she said. "It's perfectly legal."

"I am a pretty legalistic guy." Something shifted in her expression, arousing his curiosity.

"I'm glad." A wide smile lit her face. "So tell me about this house on the island."

"The owner wants to travel and doesn't want the upkeep of a big, expensive summer place. I tried to convince him to rent it out, but he didn't go for the idea. The house is a good investment—though I couldn't touch it."

"Expensive?"

He nodded. "You can say that again."

"I've seen a few of them on carriage rides. The homes there are beautiful." As if struck by a thought, Tess straightened her back. "Are you sure the ferries are running this time of year?"

"On a shortened schedule. I checked. In a couple weeks they shut down for the winter." He lifted the drink and took a sip. "I'll go one of these afternoons."

"I've never been to the island in autumn."

"Really?" An idea popped into his head, and he began devising the right way to invite her to come along without scaring her off.

"Nothing like the fragrance of autumn leaves." She drew in a lengthy breath as if imagining the aroma. "The city wears me out. So many responsibilities. So many people. So much noise. I love it here. It's the place I recharge my spirit. I burrow into nature and draw in a healing breath of fresh air and sunshine."

His pulse lurched at her intense gaze. "I think it draws me closer to what's important." He struggled to put it in words. "Like how small we are in comparison to the universe. Nature brings God into perspective.''

"Yes, I suppose it does." Her gaze moved across his face as if wondering whether he really meant what he said. Then she grinned. "That was rather poetic."

"Now you've learned my secret," he said. "Are you a poet?" His playful question triggered a new one. "What do you do for a living? I never asked."

"Nothing as glamorous as a poet. I'm a school secretary. I have to get special dispensation to come up to close this place."

Ryan laughed at her humor. "That sounds almost religious." Embarrassed, he fought a yawn and eyed his watch. "It's quarter to eleven."

"That late?" She flexed her wrist, checking the time for herself and realizing her headache had vanished.

"I'd better go." He rose and grasped his cup. "I'll help you clean up."

"No, don't be silly. Two cups and two plates are nothing. I enjoyed your company."

"Same here," he said, carrying his mug to the kitchen counter anyway.

He hadn't heard her follow him. But when he turned, she stood close enough to feel her warm breath on his skin. The hairs rose on the nape of his neck, and the tingle glided down his arms.

He raised his hands to her shoulders, bracing himself from running into her, but at the same time wanting to hold her in his arms. "Thanks for the goodies.'' He hesitated wanting to say so much more. ''I'll see you again?'' His eyes sought hers for a positive response.

Her lips curved to a smile. ''It's a small beach. I wouldn't be surprised.''

Tess offered her hand, and he took it in lieu of making a fool of himself by taking her in his arms. She walked with him, waiting while he put on his jacket and pulled the flashlight from his pocket. When she opened the door, he stepped outside into the nippy breeze.

''Good night,'' she said.

''Sweet dreams.'' The words left him before he could squelch the Romeo monologue wending its way through his thoughts. If she wouldn't laugh, he'd be quoting Shakespeare's ''parting is such sweet sorrow'' line.

He gave her a nod, and heard another ''Good night'' echoing down the slope as he followed the starlit path to the beach. He longed to rush back and ask her more about her husband's death and tell her the details of his broken engagement. The urge startled him.

When he turned to wave, her slender silhouette remained in the open doorway. He forced his feet to continue along the sand.

Chapter Three

Sunlight peeked through a gap in the bedroom curtain, and Tess opened her eyes. For a moment she forgot where she was. When she remembered, a smile rose to her lips. She was recalling the handsome intruder.

For the first time since Al's death, Tess enjoyed being with a man. Maybe because she knew Ryan's sister, one of the most down-to-earth, witty people she'd ever met.

Ryan had come from a loving family, that was sure. One of Tess's mother's adages drifted into her mind. *An acorn doesn't fall far from the tree.* He'd been open about his ended engagement. She suspected he was a man she could trust. Maybe her earlier attitude about men had been skewed. Perhaps one day she could find a man who valued family and home as much as she did.

Thinking back to Ryan's admission about looking

through people's houses, she laughed. Honest and candid. She liked that.

Tess swung her legs over the edge of the bed as an icy shiver crept through her body. Heat. She needed to turn on the wall heater or light logs in the fireplace. With speed, she dressed in sweatpants and shirt, then pulled on thick stockings and slid her feet into hiking boots.

As she opened the bedroom door, a disturbance vaulted from the living room, followed by a nerve-racking crash. Her heart leaped, and she tore down the hallway in time to see a squirrel scramble up one side of her draperies and then skitter down the other. Like a dunce, she'd forgotten to close the doors on the fireplace.

Dashing to the front door, she flung it open, but the critter flew past her and headed down the hall to the bedroom. Tess stood on the threshold, trying to decide which way to turn—go after the animal or pray it left the premises on its own. She didn't want to get bitten, but—

A hand grasped her shoulder, and a scream tore from her throat.

Ryan realized too late she hadn't heard him. As she flung her arms in frightened defense, he dodged her thrashing elbows until reality settled in and she seemed to get herself under control.

Her hand flew to her mouth, her face white. "It's—"

"Tess, I'm sorry. I thought you heard me."

"Oh, no. It's…" Her quivering voice dwindled.

Ryan's heart melted. He wrapped an arm around her shoulder, and she buried her cheek against his jacket. He tilted his head downward, looking into her frightened, frustrated face. "What's wrong?"

"A squirrel. It's in the cabin."

"A squirrel? Inside?" He nearly laughed, seeing the fear in her eyes. "Let's see what I can do." He squeezed her shoulder and bounded through the doorway.

But as he stepped inside, the creature darted between his legs, out the doorway and skittered up a tree, leaving him off balance and surprised.

Ryan pivoted toward Tess and chuckled. "He *was* inside."

She covered her face and peeked at him with one amused eye. "I feel so foolish. You must think I'm a pest."

"The squirrel's a pest, and he's left the building. You—you're just—"

"Don't tell me." She gave him a relieved grin. "I'll imagine something wonderful."

"You don't have to imagine." Ryan stepped from the doorway to her side. "Listen, Ms. Wonderful, here's a deal. Have you had breakfast?"

"Look at me." She spread her arms shoulder high. "Do I look like I've eaten? I woke to this commotion. I haven't had a thing, including a shower."

"Okay, here's the plan. Coffee's perking as we speak."

"Hmm. Coffee." She lifted her shoulders. "And I haven't grocery shopped yet."

"Get ready and come down to my place. Breakfast's in thirty minutes."

"I didn't expect this trip to prove so interesting," she called over her shoulder as she turned back into the cabin.

Ryan gave her a wave and strode down the path to the beach, his stomach empty but his mind full.

The waves lapped to the shore, and two pieces of driftwood floated onto the beach, caught together by the rolling force. A feeling of destiny wove through his conscience, as if he and Tess, like the driftwood, had been pushed together for some reason that Ryan had yet to understand.

He hoped his instincts were better than in the past.

His relationship with Donna should never have been. They were too different. She longed for fun and material things while he strove for home and simplicity. He loved the quiet life. And he'd come to learn that Donna loved the social whirl.

As much as he wanted to tell her they should rethink their future, his pride and the thought of hurting Donna wouldn't let him. He'd prayed for God to give him the courage and the way to break things off easily. His prayer had been answered. Donna did it for him. Not gently, but with anger that he'd lost his spark for fun. And he had. He couldn't deny it.

After the breakup, Ryan spent weeks thinking about what he wanted in life. The answer was easy. He wanted laughter, cozy conversations, support, empathy and love—the kind of love defined in the Bible.

Last night he'd experienced laughter and cozy conversation with a woman who he suspected loved children as much as he did. Had the Lord guided him here to meet this sweet, vulnerable woman, one who needed rescuing?

He stopped a moment, hit by a new awareness. He'd made a shambles of romance so far. Maybe he was the one being rescued.

Thinking of having breakfast across the table from Tess, his stride widened and, reaching the cozy cabin, he darted inside. After tossing his jacket on a chair, Ryan marched into the galley kitchen on one side of the room and opened a cabinet.

He hadn't brought up much—eggs, cheese and bread—but Jill always had coffee and powdered cream on hand. On one shelf, a lone onion sat inside a net bag. Whispering a thanks to his sister, Ryan poured a mug of freshly brewed coffee, then went to work on the cheese-onion omelet.

Tess knocked, and when Ryan opened the door, the delicious aroma reached Tess's senses and her stomach rumbled silently. He stood in the doorway, clutching a spatula. "Hi."

"Come on in," he said.

She noticed his admiring look, one he hadn't given her earlier in her sweatpants. Stepping inside, she turned a full circle, taking in the cheery decor. "Pretty. I've never been inside."

"Thanks. I'll tell Jill."

She followed him, amazed at the compact area and

how comfortable Ryan looked in it. He flashed a grin as cheery as the daffodil place mats.

Tess leaned against the counter and spotted a telephone hanging on the wall. "Pretty fancy. A telephone up here?"

He glanced at the apparatus. "It rarely rings, but Jill worries. Afraid something will happen. You never know when you need 911. Or a pizza." He gave her a wink.

A feathery tickle rippled through her chest. "Hmm. I never thought about pizza. Do you like them?"

"Who doesn't?" He flashed another grin and gestured toward a stool. "Have a seat."

Tess took her eyes from him long enough to slide onto the chair. Ryan set a cup of fragrant coffee in front of her, pushing the sugar bowl and creamer her way.

She added a dash of cream and took a sip as she watched him put the finishing touches on breakfast. She wondered about him, his house, his interests, his beliefs—and more about his engagement. "Where do you live downstate?" Tess asked.

Standing at the stove, he spoke over his shoulder. "Rochester. Off Avon Road near Adams."

"You're kidding? I live off Adams, but in Birmingham. Coincidence, huh?" Or Providence? A prickle of gooseflesh coursed up her arms.

"Not too far," he said, handing her a plate.

Tess eyed the fluffy omelet lying in the center of a white plate bordered with yellow daisies. A stack of toast slathered with butter sat nearby. "I'm impressed."

"Good," Ryan said, joining her on the next stool.

The omelet filled her stomach and the company filled her spirit. Then with a fresh cup of coffee, Ryan led her to the sofa where she sat facing the wide expanse of a door-wall with a view of the lake where golden streaks of sunlight rippled on the steely blue water.

Tess rested her neck against the sofa back. "Thanks. That was delicious."

"You're welcome."

Ryan wandered to the sliding glass doors, seeming more thoughtful than the night before. "Looks like a nice day." He turned to face her. "Would you like to walk?"

"Sorry. I have to make a trip into town."

"I could go with you, and—"

"Thanks, but I have to stand on my own two feet once in a while."

"But they're such tiny things," he said, eyeing her sneakers.

She saw what looked like disappointment on his face. "You've bailed me out of my propane problems and my critter attack. I need to prove I can make it into town…by myself. We can walk later. How's that?"

He lifted his broad shoulders in a shrug. "Okay."

She grinned, then rose from the sofa and grasped her cup. "I'll help you with these dishes."

"No need. What's a couple of plates and cups?"

Echoing her words from the evening before, his toying smirk made her smile. "No argument there."

She set the cup on the counter. "Since you won't let me help clean up, I'll be on my way." She headed for the door, stopping long enough to pick up her jacket. "I'll see you later."

Not waiting for a response, she pulled open the door and stepped outside. Wrapping her jacket around her shoulders, she walked down the path toward the water. The wind fluttered in uneven gusts, flapping her windbreaker and sending the colorful leaves pirouetting along the ground like ballerinas.

Though the air was warm, the strong breeze pushed her along the beach, and when Tess stepped inside the cabin, she brushed her windblown hair from her eyes. She wanted to walk with Ryan. Wanted to more than she cared to admit, but she needed time to think about what she felt and what seemed to be happening.

She slid into a chair at the small table and grasped a stubby pencil and a scratch pad, listing what she needed in town—a few groceries, the newspaper. She could check out what movie was playing in Cheboygan, and she liked to do crosswords on lonely evenings.

Lonely evenings. She'd had enough of those to last a lifetime. Ryan's image sent her heart on a fluttered journey. Could she really trust a handsome man like him? Alone in the woods, he had no other women ogling him, but back home, she wondered.

Speculations marched into her thoughts. Had Ryan

cheated on his fiancée to cause the breakup? Her chest tightened at the question. Maybe the woman had cheated on him. She shook her head. Not everyone cheated on someone…and not Ryan, she felt sure. Anyway, she hoped.

She pushed her worries aside and tended to the list. Soda, milk, eggs—she might pay back Ryan for the tasty breakfast—pancake mix, sausage. She rose and reached under the sink for a bag of returnable soda cans. Setting them on the counter, she slipped on her jacket, grabbed her shoulder bag and locked the cabin.

Outside, she got into her car and turned the key in the ignition. The motor purred to life and she shifted into reverse, but before Tess moved, she stopped, remembering she'd forgotten the sack of used cans.

Tess slid from the seat, slammed the door and darted back to the cabin, then halted. She needed keys to get into the cabin. Where was her mind? Addled by her distraction, she retraced her steps and tugged the door handle.

Locked.

Her heart sank. She looked through the window at her keys dangling from the ignition switch. Her car door locked, its motor running. Her cabin door also locked.

She pursed her lips, controlling her frustration. So this was standing on her own two feet. Two *tiny* feet. She faced her only option.

Ryan.

Chapter Four

Pushing her fists into her sides, Tess spun around and looked toward the beach. Again she felt useless and incapable. Where had her skills gone? Her ability to keep track of things? To organize? Only Ryan's reaction made her smile. She could imagine his laugh when she asked for his help again.

When she reached the water, Ryan came into view. He lifted his hand in a wave.

"Ryan," she called, cupping her hands around her mouth like a megaphone.

For a moment, she thought the waves had covered her voice. Finally, he hurried toward her. A teasing grin spread across his face and he poked himself in the chest. "Did you call me?"

Tess gazed into the sparkling green eyes and heard his chuckle rise on the wind.

"My keys," she said, pointing up the hill. She turned and led the way to her car.

"Tess, you have a gift," he said beside her.

She eyed him over her shoulder. "A gift?"

"A gift for getting into trouble."

She cringed, unable to find a snappy comeback. But the good humor in his eyes soothed her, and she slowed and fell into step at his side.

The car motor idled softly as they approached. Ryan peered inside. The scent of leather drifted from his lightweight calfskin jacket. A soft guttural "hmm" left his throat. "No problem," he said.

She thought of her extra set of keys at home. "No problem for you. Big one for me."

"Not anymore."

She gazed at his silhouette backed by the bright sun and shielded her eyes. "What do you mean?"

He held up an index finger. "Wait a minute." With a fast jog, he darted down the path and vanished around the line of trees.

Tess waited and soon he returned, carrying a long metal wire, and slid the gadget down along the window to the inner mechanism.

She watched while he manipulated the contraption, pulling and tugging. "Do those things really work?"

He peered at her over his shoulder. "Always." Withdrawing the gadget, he gave her a feeble smile and went at it again.

His feet shifted from side to side, and from behind, Tess watched his antics, admiring his wiggle, moving this way and that.

But his confidence seemed to fade while the door remained locked.

About the time she'd given up on his efforts, the lock clicked.

He turned to her. "Nothing to it."

"I can see that," she said, freeing the laughter she'd contained.

He stepped aside as she slid into the seat.

She peered into his face. "Thanks. I'm—"

"Don't say a word," he said. "Glad I could help. You only delayed my quiet, peaceful walk for a couple of minutes." He shut her door and, with a quick wave, turned and headed down the path.

Waiting before pulling away, she watched him stride toward the water and chuckled at the memory of his wiggling two-step. As he disappeared around the bend of trees, a sense of loneliness pervaded her. She pushed the feeling aside and shifted into reverse.

The soda cans.

Tess laughed to herself, turned off the motor, pulled the keys from the ignition and headed for the returnables.

She had a gift, he'd said. Well, he had one, too. The gift to solve her problems, and even more, the gift to make her feel like a woman again.

She lifted her eyes to the blue sky and spoke. "Are you up there, God? Is this your doing or am I being duped again?"

No answer came back, except a feeling in her heart that Ryan was one of God's gifts.

Tess put the last dish away and turned toward Ryan, amazed how close they'd gotten in four days.

"Thanks for wiping."

"Thanks for dinner," he said, his hip resting against the kitchen counter.

"Least I could do…for all your help these past couple of days." Truly, he was helping her again. Helping her feel less lonely and less useless.

"It was nothing. I'm getting used to digging you out of trouble." He sent her a broad smile.

"I hope it's the last time I need you.…" Though it was meant to be funny, the words faded away. She liked being with him. Just didn't like needing him.

"Don't worry. It's my turn now," he said, closing the distance between them.

Tess looked into his devilish eyes, her heart in her throat, wondering if he were going to kiss her.

"You owe me a walk. You're good at distracting me from my walks—last Friday and then Saturday when you locked your keys in the car. Remember?"

She teetered backward, disappointed. "A walk? But it'll be dark soon."

He grinned and brushed a strand of hair from her cheek. "I was walking late on Friday when I scared you to death. I like to walk in the moonlight."

Moonlight. She averted his eyes. For some foolish reason, she'd anticipated a kiss, and she prayed he didn't see the flush of mortification on her cheeks. "I— Why not? Sure. I'll get my jacket. If we hurry, we'll be back before dark." She brushed past him and grabbed a sweater.

Ryan followed behind her, seemingly unaware of

her disappointment. After slipping on his jacket, he opened the door and motioned to her.

They walked side by side down the path. The wind whipped her hair, and Ryan laughed at her hopeless struggle.

When they reached the water, they paused. White-caps rolled to shore, and Tess's gaze followed the horizon where a large steamer headed for Lake Michigan. For the third time, the thought of selling the cabin pinched her heart. She would miss the place if she did.

A tear rolled down her cheek from the nippy wind—or was it sadness? She had spent so many happy and restful summers on this beach.

"Let's head toward the creek," Ryan said, linking his arm to hers.

Tess loved the feeling of togetherness. So often her heart floated on waves of abandonment, sinking and rising, then sinking again. But today she strolled beside Ryan, talking about the shuttered cottages and other unimportant things.

Ryan squeezed her arm and drew her closer. "This is none of my business…but I'm curious. Tell me about Al. What happened?"

Her legs weakened and her ankle turned in the sand. Ryan's strong grasp steadied her.

"Watch those sand drifts," he said, not realizing his question had caused her to stumble.

Ryan had been so kind the past four days, she felt she owed him some kind of explanation, but what? She couldn't tell him the whole story. "He had worked late again…and I suppose he was tired. It was winter, and a car spun out. He swerved to avoid it…and that was it.''

"I'm sorry, Tess.'' He released her arm and slid it around her back, drawing her closer. ''What about the other passenger?''

She faltered as her body went rigid. ''The other passenger?'' Somehow he knew she'd avoided the truth.

"I meant the other driver.'' His eyes filled with question.

She contained her anxiety. ''Not a scratch.'' Why had she presumed he knew the truth?

"Well, thank the Good Lord for that,'' Ryan said, taking a step and picking up their pace.

Tess turned her face toward the water. Would life ever be the same? Though her trust had been shattered with her husband's death, Tess liked being married—sharing, dreaming and loving. Maybe it was all a fairy tale. But when she turned her head again, a pair of spring green eyes looked at her with tenderness, making her wonder if fairy tales could come true.

When they reached the creek that emptied into Lake Huron, the sun lay on the horizon, spreading vivid coral and muted lavender across the water like spilled paint. The Mackinac Bridge lights came on, tiny specks outlining the powerful cables.

"Time to go back,'' Ryan said, swinging them around to start the return walk.

"I don't mean to be so quiet,'' Tess said.

"I think I upset you with my question. I'm sorry."

"It's much more than that," Tess said, wanting so badly to trust him. "Anyway, it's your turn to tell me about your fiancée."

"Ex-fiancée."

"Okay. Ex."

Her step lightened, and she swung to collect a piece of driftwood. Ryan crouched down to gather a handful of flat stones. With each step, he skipped them across the water until the concentric ripples disappeared into a darkening sky.

"Look what I found," he said, slipping one of the pebbles into Tess's hand.

She opened her palm and stared at the smooth, pink, heart-shaped stone. Her chest tightened, and she looked into Ryan's eyes, wondering if God had sent her a sign.

When she extended her hand to return the stone, Ryan shook his head. "Keep it."

She slid the rock into her pocket, keeping her hand there to run her fingers over the rounded edges.

"It's dark already," Ryan said, pulling a flashlight from his pocket and sending a beam of light onto the path.

"You think of everything."

"Walking without a light is asking for trouble."

Avoiding the shadowy ruts, Tess clung to Ryan's side. Silver dots shimmered across the water and a round moon glowed with ruffled edges on the rippling waves. She stopped before walking back up the hill to the cabin.

"I have two things to say," she said.

"Two?"

Tess couldn't see his face, but she heard concern in his voice. She grinned into the darkness. "First, thanks for the walk. It was fun,"

"And second?"

"You haven't answered my question about your ex-fiancée, and I expect an answer."

Ryan stood in front of the fireplace clasping a steaming mug and gazed at Tess, his thoughts banging in his head like bumper cars. But one thought stood out from the rest. "I find you very attractive, Tess."

Her eyes widened before she laughed. "You'll say anything to avoid talking about 'what's her name.'"

"Donna," he said, feeling uneasy mentioning Donna while his mind was filled with Tess. "I meant what I said. I might as well confess I thought you were a beautiful woman years ago when we met…but you were married and I'm a man of honor." *Honor.* The word prickled through him. If he'd been an honorable man, he'd have ended his relationship with Donna long before she did.

Tess's gaze shifted from him to the dancing flames and remained silent. Then when she faced him, she studied his face before speaking. "I find you appealing, too, Ryan…but we barely know each other and—"

"Please don't get me wrong, Tess. I'm not suggesting anything intimate. I just wanted you to know how I feel.''

He took a step forward and settled on the edge of the same overstuffed chair he always sat in.

Tess shifted, a look of confusion growing on her face, her eyes riveted to Ryan's as if trying to seek some deeper truth.

''Donna and I had mutual friends and some common interests, but after the engagement I noticed a change...maybe in both of us. Donna didn't seem to want to settle down.'' He rubbed his neck. ''I had the feeling that she liked the idea of having a husband, but not the idea of being a wife.''

Tess frowned.

''My view of marriage is two people having a family and sharing their lives,'' he said. ''I pictured us sitting around talking...like we are right now. Conversation, laughter, talking about nature and God. Donna doesn't sit still long enough to have a conversation. I thought that would change once a commitment was made but—''

''Commitments don't mean the same thing to people,'' Tess said, her eyes filled with so much sadness, Ryan puzzled at what it meant.

''That's true...and I suppose people don't really change. We just misread each other for a while.''

His chest tightened when he saw sadness in Tess's eyes. ''What is it, Tess? Did I say something to upset you?''

She shook her head. ''Sorry,'' she mumbled, wiping the stray tears from her cheek. "I was just thinking how awful life can be sometimes."

"Awful sometimes, but wonderful most often. And when things are really difficult we have God."

"But what if God doesn't have us?"

Her despondent gaze sent a chill through him. "I've lost a fiancée, but never a spouse. I can only imagine how horrible that must be."

He rose and knelt beside her, taking her hand in his. "God doesn't give up on us, Tess. The Lord is with us always, but sometimes our cries aren't answered the way we think they should be. In time, we understand."

She nodded, then withdrew her hand from his and caressed his cheek. "So why do you feel guilty about Donna?"

"I should have been more honest with her. I prayed that God give me a way to end the relationship...." He couldn't help but grin. "And then when she did, I was shocked."

For the first time since the conversation began, Tess smiled. "So she hurt your pride."

He nodded. And he began singing "Macho Man."

"Thanks for being honest," she said. She took a sip of tea. "It's cold."

Rising from his crouched position, Ryan took her mug and his, then carried them to the kitchen. He wondered if he'd ever know what had hurt her so deeply. She called him honest, but he'd avoided some things he shouldn't have. He just wasn't ready.

"Did you notice the orange sunset tonight?" he

said, moving toward the doorway. "Looks like we'll have a nice day. Remember...red sky at night, sailor's delight." He spun around to face her. "Why not come to Mackinac Island with me tomorrow? I think the weather will be perfect."

Tess stood and ambled toward him. "I haven't been there in years. It might be fun."

"I suppose the bike rentals are closed for the season," he said, "but we can hire a horse and buggy. Checking the house shouldn't take too long. We might even have time for dinner there. What do you say?"

"I say yes." She reached up and patted his cheek.

When she pulled back, he captured her gaze, fighting the desire to kiss her.

Chapter Five

The horse's *clip-clop* echoed in the quiet of the Tuesday afternoon. The buggy rocked, side to side, as they descended the hill back into town.

"I told you the assessment would be fast," Ryan said, taking advantage of the weather to slide his arm around Tess's shoulder. "If he wants to sell, I'll have to contact an assessor in the area for him, but at least I can give him an idea of value."

"The house is magnificent. I can't understand the man wanting to give it up."

"Me, neither," Ryan said, thinking how magnificent she looked in the late-afternoon sun. "Any place like this with a view of the water and sky…and on an island is priceless. But so is your place."

"The cabin?"

"I bet you don't have the foggiest idea how much your place is worth."

She turned toward him, her brow creased in question. "Well?" She lifted a brow.

He gave her shoulder a squeeze. "Lakefront property is valuable…and *good* lakefront like yours is hard to come by. Let's see. You probably have two hundred feet of waterfront. I'd guess the land alone is worth more than a hundred thousand."

"A hundred thousand? You're kidding."

"Nope."

Though she drew his attention toward Fort Mackinac as the carriage rattled past, Tess grew quiet, a sullen thoughtfulness that made Ryan feel alone. Ahead, Main Street stretched in each direction and beyond the glinting water of the Straits of Mackinac.

"Dollar for your thoughts," he said.

A moment passed before she faced him. "I've been wondering."

"About?"

"The cabin. You just mentioned how much it's worth, and that's a coincidence, because I've been thinking that I should sell the place.…" Her voice faded, leaving an echoing sadness.

"Sell it? But why, Tess? You've said so often how much the cabin means to you." Her face told the story. She didn't want to sell the property.

"I can't keep it up myself—not the way I should—and hiring out the work is too expensive. Besides, I'm lonely here by myself."

"It can get lonely, I know." He'd planned to be alone these past days and realized now how wonderful the time had been with Tess. Not just filling his hours, but helping him realize what a relationship should really be. His gaze drifted heavenward, and again, he wondered if this were the Lord's way of guiding his life.

Tess remained quiet, and Ryan withdrew from his own thoughts, realizing she struggled with her decision.

"Don't rush into anything, Tess. Think about it over the winter. If you decide, you can sell the place next spring."

She stared off toward the horizon. "I'm sure you're right."

With his arm around her shoulder, Ryan felt a shiver course through her. He squeezed her arm to assure her. Then he followed the direction of her eyes to the distance.

The sun had begun to set beyond the length of the Mackinac Bridge, and the colors melted together— yellow to orange to red to purple. Awesome and unreal.

He felt a tremor through her shoulders. "It's beautiful," she murmured.

Mesmerized by the moment, he could only nod. When his gaze shifted from the sun's display to Tess's glowing face, the sight took his breath away. The sun played on her deep brown hair, and her cheeks glowed with the colors gracing the horizon. Ryan prayed the excitement on her face stemmed, in a small way, from sharing the day with him.

Tess felt Ryan's stare, and the heat of a flush burned her cheeks. She wondered if he felt as drawn to her as she to him. From the moment they met, she sensed kinship between them. He made her laugh and feel complete, and gentleness flowed from beneath his handsome, rugged demeanor.

The buggy rumbled and rocked as it turned the corner, maneuvering from the asphalt to the cement of the main roadway. The driver pulled to the curb, and Ryan leaped out first and lifted her to the ground. With him, a feeling of femininity came alive again. Something she thought had vanished.

After he paid the driver, they took a few steps and paused at one of the shops. "Not much open. Want to look here?" Ryan asked.

"Sure. I might buy myself a sweatshirt." Buying a memento took on an unexpected importance. Tess would have something tangible to remember the wonderful days they'd shared.

Inside the shop, a sweatshirt caught Tess's eye. She loved the muted teal with the bridge imprinted on a swash of colorful sunset, very close to the glorious sight they'd witnessed on their ride back into town. "Look."

Ryan wandered to her side as she selected the size.

"We're ready to close," the saleswoman called from the checkout. "Did you want that?"

Tess nodded and carried the shirt to the clerk.

The woman glanced at the price and punched keys on the cash register. She opened a shopping bag and dropped the shirt and wire hanger inside.

Tess handed her the bills, and the young woman

laid the change into her hand with a grin. "Honey-mooners? I can always spot them."

Heat crept up Tess's neck. "No. Just visiting. We're taking the ferry back tonight."

The woman's eyebrows lifted. "I hope you're kidding. The ferry left at six. It's a long swim back."

Ryan's mouth dropped open as he glanced at his watch. "You're joking."

"No, it's five after right now. You may catch it if you run like the wind."

Tess's heart thudded. "What do you think?"

Ryan grabbed her hand. "I think we'd better run for it."

They bolted from the building and down the sidewalk toward the dock, but a sharp kink caught in Tess's side, and she slowed.

"Go ahead." She pressed her fingers against the stabbing pain before darting on again.

Ryan faltered, then ran ahead and turned the corner, vanishing beyond the building that blocked a view of the pier.

Tess pushed herself forward, her legs stretching as she rounded the corner, her feet resounding on the heavy planks.

But when she lifted her eyes, Ryan stood alone on the pier, the ferry a silhouette heading for the city. He shrugged and headed back her way.

"What will we do now?" Tess asked.

"Look at the bright side. We have time to enjoy dinner on the island."

A mixture of panic and intrigue filtered through Tess. Dinner, then what? They were stranded.

He grasped her arm and steered her back to Main Street. When their feet hit the concrete, Ryan paused and looked up one side and down the other, then glanced at his watch. "I suppose we should find a place to stay first. Not much is open."

He slid his arm around her shoulders and turned left in the direction of the Grand Hotel. Looking at their garb—jeans, knit shirts, and jackets—Tess laughed.

"I'm glad you can find humor in this," Ryan said.

"I was thinking that even if the Grand Hotel has rooms, we couldn't stay there. Guests have to dress up after six."

He grinned. "I saw a sign at the ferry landing. Bay View Inn is still open."

"We hope." Chilled by the nippy air, she gave in to her desire and snuggled closer to his side.

They walked in silence, gasping against a heavy breeze and the inclined sidewalk. Relieved, yet flustered, Tess spotted the yellow-and-white Victorian building adorned with an oval sign, Bay View Inn.

They climbed the steps to the wide wraparound porch lined with white wicker rocking chairs. Tess held back while Ryan opened the door and strode inside to the tinkle of a bell.

He looked at Tess over his shoulder, and she forced herself to enter, too aware of their lack of luggage and their embarrassing situation.

The clerk came through a doorway, and Tess listened while Ryan explained their situation. The clerk's eyes shifted from Tess to Ryan as if wondering how they could be so stupid.

"We'd like two rooms," Ryan said, ending his wary tale.

The clerk shook his head. "We're about filled. There's a large conference at the Grand." His fingers pecked at the computer keys. "All I have is one queen. Oh…and the Premiere Suite." His gaze raked over their attire.

Ryan glanced at Tess over his shoulder. "What do you think?"

Tess shrugged, imagining the cost. "Premiere Suite? Wouldn't that be expensive?"

The clerk looked at her over his spectacles. "Three hundred plus tax."

"For one night?" Tess asked, realizing neither of them wanted to spend hundreds of dollars for their stupid mistake. "No exceptions?"

"None," the clerk said.

"Are any other inns open?" Ryan asked overlapping the man's response.

"The Grand Hotel," the clerk said, again eyeing their attire, "but I don't think—"

"What's the rate for the room with a queen," Tess asked, irritated with the man's attitude.

"One hundred and seventy-five dollars."

Tess lifted her shoulders and drew in a deep breath. "We'll take it."

Ryan faced her. "Are you sure?"

She nodded and managed a look of confidence

while concern rattled through her like a bag of marbles. Though she recalled Ryan's words—*"I'm not suggesting anything intimate"*—could she trust him tonight?

Could she trust herself?

After dinner at the Calico Pony, Tess stood in the doorway and eyed the room she had to share with Ryan. She gazed at the Victorian decor. The four-poster, queen-size bed was covered in an old-fashioned quilt and there was a chintz-covered easy chair with ottoman in the corner.

Sensing Ryan behind her, Tess stepped into the room and dropped her shoulder bag and sweatshirt sack on the oak vanity table.

Ryan moved past her, crossed to the lace-curtained windows where darkness pushed against the pane and pulled the shade. When he pivoted toward Tess, she struggled with a this-is-too-intimate sensation that charged through her.

"Now what?" he asked.

Tess shook her head, not knowing what he expected her to say. She wanted to remind him about his comment about no intimacy, but it seemed out of place with his simple question.

Instead, Tess eyed her watch, then assured the time by looking at the digital alarm on the nightstand. "Try to rest, I suppose."

He nodded and swung his hand toward the bed. "You take the bed, and I'll use the chair."

She looked at the small chair and shook her head,

but he ignored her, moving past to snatch a pillow from the bed and heading across the room.

He kicked off his shoes, adjusted the ottoman under his legs and leaned his head back against the pillow.

Tess chuckled at the picture. His long legs and feet extended beyond the footstool and he looked miserable. "This is ridiculous, Ryan. I'm smaller. You take the bed." She snapped on the bedside light and waited.

"No gentleman allows a woman to sleep in a chair while he takes the bed." He pushed the ottoman away from the chair to catch more of his leg. "This is fine. Comfortable."

His "comfortable" position looked awkward, but she stopped arguing and stepped across the room to bolt the door and turn off the larger light. When she returned to the bed, she loosened her belt, slipped off her shoes and stretched out on the top of the quilt before glancing at Ryan who had closed his eyes, his hands folded in his lap, his head tilted back.

"Good night," she said, and snapped off the light.

She felt miserable without a toothbrush or clean change of clothing, but Ryan looked more pitiable twisted into the chair.

Darkness shrouded the room, and Tess held her breath and listened to Ryan's even breathing. He'd been true to his word. Not one sexual overture. Not even a joke about them being alone in the room.

Feeling a chill settle over her, Tess rose and climbed beneath the blanket, but soon her thoughts shifted to Ryan. Fearing he'd be cold, she stood again and pulled off the spread, then with moonlight streaming in from the edge of the window shade, she carried the quilt to his chair and draped it over him.

"You didn't have to do that," he said.

Hearing the nearness of his gentle voice sent her heart dipping to her stomach before fluttering upward to repose where it belonged. "It's getting cold."

"Thanks, Tess."

In the moonlight through a chink between the wall and shade, she saw him tuck the quilt beneath his chin and nestle down again.

Tess returned to the bed, but her mind felt as agitated as Ryan appeared hanging between the chair and ottoman.

Under cover of night, Tess longed to open her heart and talk to Ryan about the things she'd struggled with for so many years. Though her family knew the details of Al's death, she'd held back the greater fears that scarred her heart. But these past days, she'd let God's presence and Ryan fill her thoughts, and the new hope helped to dislodge the anger and hurt that had adhered so tightly to her emotions.

Rolling on her side, Tess gazed at Ryan's outline in the darkness. His silhouette had grown familiar and comforting. Today, unknowingly, he'd proved himself honorable and trustworthy.

The shadowed form shifted in the chair, and before Tess's eyes, the chair and ottoman parted company while Ryan thumped to the floor between them.

He released a loud "oomph" and struggled to rise, tangled in ottoman and quilt.

Tess flung her legs from the bed and snapped on the light. She watched him free himself and settle his feet on the floor, an embarrassed look covering his face. She couldn't help but laugh. Yet her mind and heart knew that he'd done everything tonight to show her respect. He'd honored her morals and beliefs. Beneath Tess's chuckle her declaration rang with sincerity. "Enough, Ryan."

"I'm sorry, Tess."

"No," she said, walking toward him and grabbing the spread from the floor. "Enough of this silliness."

She returned to the bed and threw the quilt to the other side.

"Come here and get some rest."

Chapter Six

Ryan faltered, squinting in the brightness and wondering if he were sleeping and this were all a dream. Since they'd agreed on the sleeping arrangements, he'd questioned how he'd get through the next ten hours holed up with Tess in the same hotel room. "You sure about this?"

Tess patted the mattress. "I'm sure. If you wanted to ravage me, you'd have done it already."

He brushed his hair from his forehead and ambled around the bed to the opposite side. "You sound pretty sure of yourself."

"I am." She grinned and slid her legs beneath the blanket. Turning on her side, Tess snapped off the bed lamp.

The mattress dipped as Ryan settled onto the bed, spreading out beside her and leaving a cautious space between them.

She lay there, still and silent, her back to him in the dim moonlight.

Ryan tried to push away his thoughts. Instead his senses aroused knowing he was so close beside Tess. His thoughts tossed in his head, and though his body cried out for sleep, his mind was relentless. He eased up and peered at the red digital numbers, then rolled on his back and stared at the inky ceiling.

"Ryan," she whispered.

He shifted and rolled in slow motion toward her. "Tess?"

"I'm thinking."

"Thinking?"

"That I lied to you today." She turned toward him and raised herself on an elbow.

"You lied?"

"Not lied exactly...but I didn't tell you the whole truth."

His chest tightened with speculation. He joined her, propped on his elbow with his head against his fist.

"What do you mean?"

"It's about Al's death."

He held his breath, feeling the mattress stir as she neared him.

"It's true he died in a car accident," she said.

He sucked in air.

"But he wasn't alone." Her voice filled with sadness.

Ryan's imagination flew. Had Tess been with him? Had she been driving? Sorrow shot through him, and he leaned toward her and his hand touched hers. "Oh, Tess. You were in the—"

"He died with another woman in the car," Tess said.

"Another woman?" The words spun in his thoughts. "You mean—"

"He'd been having an affair. For all those years, he'd been saying he had to work and…"

Ryan lifted his hand toward her face to brush her cheek. Her grief became his. Emotions expanded in his chest. Anger, frustration, sorrow for Tess, pain for her suffering.

"I'm so sorry, Tess."

"I don't love him anymore, Ryan. I'm just mortified that I lived in ignorance for so long."

He edged closer and drew Tess to his side. She didn't pull away, but rested her head against his shoulder.

"I didn't have an inkling. I felt…humiliated. So stupidly gullible. I believed his excuses. The typical ones—working late, entertaining clients, out-of-town conferences. Can you believe how stupid I was?"

"Don't say that, Tess. Why would you doubt him? When you love someone, you trust them. Marriage means a promise of commitment and faithfulness. Why would you think otherwise?"

His body twinged with the hurt he felt coursing through her.

"But there were too many clues. He grew distant. Distracted, not interested in…me. Quick kisses, mundane conversation. I believed him. I trusted him. I was faithful to him. And I was naive."

Ryan caressed her arm and nestled his head against hers. "You weren't naive, Tess. Love means trust. They go hand in hand."

"That's what I always thought," she said.

Her mouth lay so close, he felt the brush of her breath against his face. He struggled with the deepest desire to take her in his arms and kiss away her sadness, but she'd spoken of broken trust. Any action now would destroy the faith she had in him.

Instead, Ryan pressed his finger against her lips, then drew his hand to her head and petted her hair, soothing her to stillness.

Minutes passed before her breathing steadied and deepened. Ryan held her in his arms, watching the sun rise through a small crevice between the window frame and the shade.

The morning sun glinted on the water, and Tess went ahead of Ryan up the ramp onto the ferry. She'd slept fitfully, awakening to find herself in Ryan's arms—her body beneath the sheet and he on top of the blanket, covered by the quilt.

The feeling of longing overwhelmed her. The yearning to be complete and whole again. The desire to be in the arms of a man who loved her as much as she loved him.

In the morning light, her feelings for Ryan frightened her. She'd grown to care for him. His tenderness and honesty had broken down her barriers of fear, and she recalled seeing him over the past years. During that time, Tess had observed Ryan with Davie, enjoying their relationship. She saw love in the child's eyes as he looked at his uncle, and Ryan's gaze brimmed with love and delight, as he'd play with the boy on the beach.

She remembered that sunny day and recalled her admiration grew for Ryan, a man she barely knew, who seemed so devoted to his family. Though a sin, she envied him.

Before the miscarriages, she'd envisioned Al a family man. But after she miscarried, once, twice, Al seemed to change, and she'd missed that kind of loving she'd seen in Al's eyes—the kind of look Ryan gave her even talking about Davie. She'd longed for that kind of family love.

During breakfast at the inn, Ryan had been quiet. He'd made no comment about her confession the night before, but she noticed his eyes looked tired. She wondered if he'd lain awake worrying about her…or worse, pitying her. Still she'd told him the truth—most of the truth—and the confession gave her relief.

Aboard the ferry, Ryan guided her to a seat inside the cabin, and she sat close to him, watching the city grow nearer during the fifteen-minute ride back to Mackinaw City.

When they left the ferry, only a few cars stood in the parking lot. Even the streets remained quiet with shops not opening until ten o'clock.

Contentment lingered in Tess's thoughts as they

headed for Ryan's car. As they approached, he dug through his pockets for the car keys, then stopped and felt again. His hands dropped to his sides, and he looked at Tess with an embarrassed grin. "Guess what?"

"Hmm?"

"No keys."

"You're kidding." From his expression, she knew he wasn't.

Ryan looked through the car window and pointed. His expression was more amused than amazed. "Serves me right for being such as smart aleck."

Though she'd thought it, Tess didn't rub it in. "You can open the door with that thingamabob."

He raised his eyebrows and stared at her with a wry grin. "My thingamabob's in the trunk. And guess what?"

She fought the grin that spread across her face. "You need the key."

"How'd you guess? And wipe that silly grin off your face." He gave her a teasing poke.

Sharing a lighthearted moment in the midst of the recent turmoil felt wonderful. They stood staring at the car in amused silence.

He shrugged. "We'd better find a gas station. It's a long walk to the cabins."

"How's your thumb?" Tess tossed her shoulder bag and package on the trunk of the car, planning a comic hitchhike demonstration. As the bag hit the lid, a dull tink sounded. Then she remembered. The sweatshirt hanger. "Listen, Mr. Rescuer, what would you give me for a solution to your problem?"

His brows knitted. "What do you mean?"

"Maybe I can solve your problem for once."

"Don't get my hopes up."

"No. Seriously."

"Okay. I'll buy you dinner tonight."

Better than she hoped. Tess gave him a teasing grin, dug into her shopping bag and pulled out the metal clothes hanger. "Voilà."

His face shifted from curious to relieved. He grasped the wire from her hands. "But if this doesn't work, I'm off the hook for dinner."

He manipulated the hanger in his strong fingers, straightening and bending it to match the gadget he'd used earlier. After a few tense moments, he slid the wire between the door and the window pane and began his infamous wiggle. This time, Tess laughed out loud.

He eyed her over his shoulder. "What's so funny?"

"You'd have to stand behind yourself and watch." She demonstrated a little jiggle for him.

"Nice," he said, giving her a wink and turning back to his work. In a moment, he faced her. "Have a good laugh, my dear woman, because—" he swung around to show her "—the door is open." He waved his self-created door opener like a magic wand.

She caught him with an enthusiastic embrace. As she nestled against his chest, their eyes met. Longing rose in Ryan's face. His soft gaze caressed her with half-opened eyes, and her body molded to his as his arms drew her closer. She felt the hanger fall from his fingers and slide to the ground.

She stood transfixed, lost in his eyes and uncaring about some early riser who might see them. Her pulse galloped, taking her breath away. Ryan's lips neared hers, and she tiptoed to meet him, ready and eager.

His soft, supple mouth touched hers, sending a flutter through her chest. How long had it been since she'd felt a kiss this gentle, yet impassioned?

When their lips parted, Tess gazed at Ryan's face as he contemplated hers. His arms clasped her so close, she felt the beating of his heart through her jacket. Her own skipped like a child jumping rope. The urgency passed, and they relaxed in their embrace.

Ryan's eyes filled with a devilish twinkle as he spoke. "I think we'd better get out of here before we're arrested."

She allowed the light moment to pull her from the sensations coursing through her. "A few hours in jail might be good for both of us."

"Or a cold shower," Ryan said.

Ryan hung up the telephone later that day and clutched the kitchen counter to steady himself. *Donna.* He couldn't believe she'd called Jill to find out why he hadn't answered the call she'd left on his answering machine. And now, Donna had called him here.

He tilted his head back, sending up a needed prayer. *Lord, help her to understand it's over.* He stood a moment hoping to calm his fluttering heart. Why had Donna decided that their broken engagement was wrong? He knew it was right. He'd known much sooner than she had that they weren't meant for each other, but he'd give Donna time to realize it, too. And he let her break the engagement.

Today, she said, she'd had second thoughts. Not Ryan. He'd been relieved from the moment she gave him back the ring. Though he hadn't followed through, he wanted her to keep it as a gift. A thank-you for making the decision easy.

Easy. Not anymore. Today she'd made it complicated. She'd begged him to get together to talk it over. To get her to hang up, Ryan had agreed to see her when he returned. But change his mind? Never. Not before he'd found Tess and certainly not after. Tess was all that filled his mind.

Since the moment they'd met and he learned she was widowed, he sensed that God had brought them together. He knew in his heart she was the woman he'd dreamed of calling his own. The woman meant to share his life.

In a way, the revelation seemed foolish. They'd seen each other on occasion over the years, but only in the past week had they really gotten to know each other.

Ryan glanced at his watch and hurried to the car. Tess was waiting for him to take her to dinner. Now what would he do? Tell her about the call?

Though it seemed right, he didn't like the idea. She'd just begun to trust him. She'd just begun to show her feelings toward him. What would happen if he told her Donna wanted him back.

Pulling down the lane, Ryan saw Tess waiting for him. Her dark hair appeared streaked by the sunset and her olive green-and-gold jacket brightened her countenance like autumn leaves.

She slid into the car, and he paused looking at her heightened color and her warm smile. "You are beautiful, Tess."

She lowered her eyes, a deeper glow washing her cheeks. "You're not so bad yourself."

"Thanks," he said, shifting into reverse and backing around. "Let's try the Embers. I think they're still open."

The Embers was less than a mile up the highway. Though the parking lot looked empty, the Open sign glowed in the dusk from the window.

Walking beside Tess into the restaurant, Ryan knew she'd become thoughtful again. He'd gotten carried away earlier at the ferry dock, and he feared she regretted the kiss. He didn't regret it at all. Only Donna's call had set him on edge.

They found seats, and after they studied the menu, he sat back, needing to apologize. "I hope I didn't upset you this morning, Tess."

She raised her shy eyes to his. "The enthusiasm was mutual." She focused on the silverware, napkin, seemingly everything, but him. "But I don't want you to think...I have anything more...to offer. I—"

Ryan heard her words before she said them. Her anxiety was the same as his. He loved kissing her, but he meant to act with control, not like a love-starved idiot. He placed his hand on hers. "I'm sorry, Tess. My testosterone got carried away, but I'm not expecting anything more than you're willing or able to give."

"I'm more scared of my own feelings, Ryan. I've always believed in…keeping myself…for marriage. Maybe that sounds silly since I was married once, but—"

"Not silly at all."

"But this morning, I found myself wanting…" Her pale skin colored more deeply.

Ryan had felt the same. Had longed to make love to her. Had yearned to feel the softness of her body against his, but he pushed away his longings—the same as he'd controlled his desire. Instead, he needed to ease her anxiety.

"Don't feel badly, Tess. I'm no Don Juan, but I'm sure not perfect, either." He studied her face, hoping to see her tension fade. "My hormones and I've had a few battles, but my good sense usually wins out."

She shifted in her chair, then lifted her gaze and looked into his eyes. "I'm glad you understand."

He nodded.

"And it's not that I don't like you. I do."

"And I like you, too. A lot." He drew her hand to his lips enjoying the soft coolness of her fingers. They remained in a silent pose, gazes locked.

Unnoticed, the waitress arrived, and when Ryan

became aware, he looked at her and caught her grin. "Honeymooners?"

Ryan slid Tess's hand to the table with a chuckle and picked up the menu. "Only wishful thinking," he said. He eyed Tess to see her response. She blinked, then gave the flicker of a smile.

With the interruption, they ordered and regained their composure. Tess rested her cheek on her hand. "I like that about you, Ryan. You're frank and honest." A myriad of emotions swept across her face.

"I try to be," he said, swallowing his guilt in hearing her truthful comment. Tess had given him a lead to tell her about Donna's call. To admit the breakup had happened only weeks before. But he couldn't. She might not understand.

Chapter Seven

After coffee and toast the next morning, Tess headed for the beach alone. She'd sensed a difference in Ryan during dinner the past evening. What had caused it? She hoped it hadn't been the details of Al's infidelity she'd related earlier that day. Infidelity insinuated an unhealthy marriage. Did he think her an inept wife? She'd asked herself the same question. Another thought nudged her thinking. Could it have been her bluntness about chastity? She shuffled her thoughts like playing cards, turning them up to find the jokers instead of aces.

The sun glinted off the rippling waves that rolled to shore, and she moved briskly in the direction away from Ryan's cottage. She needed to think in silence. Alone.

Not only did Ryan fill her thoughts, but the cabin pressed on her mind. Since Ryan knew real estate, she wondered if she should ask him to appraise the

property and take care of the listing information—
just in case. Her "just in case" was only a balm to
ease the pain. Keeping the cabin would be foolish.
Her heart sank as she weighed her decision.

Tess picked up her pace along the moist sand. As
she jogged along the shore, her feet left imprints in
the ground. Her pulse raced, and the cool breeze
numbed her cheekbones. She tucked her hands into
her pockets to warm them, and finally, out of breath,
she slowed, then stopped. She had jogged a good
mile, and the creek lay just ahead of her.

Tess leaned down, propping her hands against her
thighs, until her heartbeat returned to normal. Pausing, her mind filled with questions. After last night,
she knew she wanted to see more of Ryan. His gentle
kiss, his tender touch lingered in her mind. She was
sure he felt the same.

But could she trust him? Was he keeping something from her? An occasional flash of unspoken concerns sparked in his eyes, then faded. Or was it her
own doubt? She wanted to believe in him. Since Al's
death, he was the first to stir her heart and her emotions.

She turned and ambled back toward the cabin. In
the distance, a person headed her way, and she knew
without question it was Ryan. As they neared, his
hand raised in a welcoming wave. She gestured back,
her pulse skipping for a moment at the sight of him.

"Morning." His voice drifted to her on the breeze.
A smile rose to her lips without effort while all her
fears faded like her footprints in the wave-washed

sand. She found her legs carrying her like the wind to his waiting arms.

"Hi," she gasped.

He wrapped her in his arms, nearly lifting her from the ground in his powerful embrace.

Her pulse raced with the joy of his touch.

"Whoa! Just holding you rattles my senses." He released her and stepped back. "What's gotten into me?"

A flush rose on her cheeks, looking into his amazed eyes. "I don't know."

"I do. *You.* You addle me. I'm putty in your hands. I'm a fool, misbehaving. Put me in a corner and give me a time-out."

"That would be safer." Tess chuckled, yet acknowledging her own behavior. "You've heard of shipboard romances. Well, it's the water. Moonlight rippling on the waves. Something like that."

"No moonlight, my love," he said, gesturing to the cheerful sky, "It's pure day, but I suppose sunlight could be the culprit, too." He drew back with the most timid, boyish expression that made her heart sing. "Could I, at least, hold your hand?"

"Only if you behave." She wanted to swallow those words, but God's will nudged her to follow her faith.

He crossed his heart with the index finger and held his hand up in a pledge. "Scout's honor."

"I've known some pretty nasty scouts in my day." She chuckled and stretched her hand to his.

Ryan grasped it, and his firm touch brought a sense

of wholeness to her empty life. They ambled, side by side, in the direction of the cabins as the sun-tipped tide washed the tangled vines and pink-hued shells around their feet.

Waves and gulls were the only sounds. They walked in comfortable silence until Tess broke the quiet. "Could you do me a favor while we're here?"

Ryan's curiosity surged. "Sure. What?"

"Could you do an appraisal on the cabin? If I decide to sell, then I'll have what I need and you could list it for me."

His anxiety subsided. He sensed Tess forcing the sale of the cabin, and he worried about her haste. "Sure, but I thought—"

"In fact, Ryan, there's no question. I need to sell the place as much as I don't want to. It's foolish to hang on to it."

He saw her defiant chin, flaunting false bravery like the night behind the cabin. "Don't make a rash decision. I'll give you a market evaluation. But wait until you're back home. I'd rather you think on it first."

Her determined voice softened. "I know, but the taxes and the upkeep are expensive, especially when the place needs repairs or a fallen tree removed. Have you ever seen what winter does to trees up here?"

Ryan wrapped his arm around her shoulder. "Ever think about a miracle?"

She raised her reticent eyes to his. Tess shook her head. "I've given up on those."

As she lowered her gaze, Ryan's mind billowed

like the rolling tide, spilling tangled thoughts at his feet. He'd rescued her before, and he longed to do it again. Anything to put a smile back on her face.

Tess tucked her arm around his waist with a gentle squeeze. "You can see I can't be here alone. First of all, I'm nearly helpless by myself. Everything that could go wrong does."

She didn't know, but he could say the same. Donna's phone call flashed before his eyes. "Things aren't always perfect for me, either. I might look competent, but things go very wrong for me, too. Don't let me fool you, Tess. I have fears just like you do." The unwelcome concerns reeled into his thoughts.

She stared at him, her expression disbelieving. Then a faint smile softened her face. "I thought you were my hero. You could save the day. What happened to that?"

He squeezed her shoulder. "I lied. Men lie all the time."

Tess flinched when the words tumbled from his mouth, and he wanted to kick himself. "I'm sorry, Tess. I was only kidding. All men don't lie. I don't."

She slowed and lifted her eyes to his. "I'm sorry. I'm too sensitive."

"I was stupid to say that."

"It's not you. It's me."

He shook his head, seeing no way to change her mind. She seemed determined to blame herself for everything, but he understood why. "Let's talk about the cabin. I've hassled you about selling it, but I really understand. Would you like me to do the appraisal now?''

''Sure, it's now or never, I suppose. I keep thinking about going home tomorrow. I suppose that's making me sad.''

Going home tomorrow. The words plummeted to his feet. Home meant saying goodbye and, then, facing Donna once again to convince her the breakup was right. The situation knotted in his stomach. He hated confrontation.

He looked at Tess's expression and realized that she suspected something was wrong. That had to be part of the problem. She knew he was keeping something from her. But how could he explain it until it was over?

On the way back from their last dinner together, Ryan had an idea. ''How about a bonfire tonight?''

''A bonfire. It sounds wonderful. You don't think it's too cold by the water?''

''Not when I have my love to keep me warm.''

His boyish charm jangled her thoughts. She'd spent the last few days fighting desire—an alien sensation these past years. Though virtue was winning, part of Tess longed for it to lose. Inside she felt the battle between passion and control. She sensed Ryan felt the same.

The road loomed before them, and Ryan turned onto a lane, nearly as hidden in the trees as her own. When they climbed from the car, he went for the beach chairs while Tess grabbed pieces of fallen limbs and headed for the beach.

Working in the dusky light, they made quick work of the fire. Ryan dragged logs from a pile at the edge of the woods. The flames licked the air, and sparks rose into the darkening sky like fireflies.

They settled in the lawn chairs, and Tess relaxed, noting the burnished leaves bursting more fully into color each day. "Autumn's my favorite time of year."

"It is? Most people prefer spring or summer."

"I know, but there's something special about autumn. Sort of a promise." Her chest tightened at memories of the past days she'd spent with Ryan. Days brightened by hope.

"I thought spring's the season of promise. Rebirth, new life—"

"No. To me, it's autumn…when you're talking about *real* life."

He rubbed his palm against her fingers resting on the arm of the lawn chair. "Real life?"

"As I see it, life isn't always perfect. Things fade and die like the leaves." She motioned to the colorful leaves floating on the breeze to the ground. "Things come to an end like life—even marriages. Hope fades. Disappointments come—cold and lonely like winter."

"Tess, you're depressing me." He lifted her fingers and pressed them to his lips.

"Don't be depressed. Remember I said autumn holds a promise. We always know after the leaves die and winter comes that sunshine and new life are around the corner.''

''Ah—spring.''

''Sure, but it all starts with autumn.''

He threaded her fingers through his. ''Autumn makes me think of Thanksgiving sort of in the same way. We give thanks for all that's gone before, knowing each year the harvest returns again.''

She squeezed his hand. ''I love Thanksgiving, too, but for a different reason. It brings loved ones together. Praising God, yes, but celebrating family as well as blessings.''

''Yes. Family.'' The sound in Ryan's voice caused her to turn. He had a faraway look in his eye that aroused Tess's curiosity.

Silence surrounded them, and Tess watched lights come up on the island and outline the bridge. As the heat grew, she pushed back from the flames and Ryan followed.

''This campfire was a great idea, Ryan. What a nice way to end our week.'' But the word *end* pierced her heart.

''It was.'' He took her hand in his and pressed her fingers to his cool lips. ''I can't believe tomorrow's Saturday already.''

''The time's been special.''

He drew her hand closer and nestled it against his jacket. ''I don't want to leave you, Tess.''

''It's been wonderful. So much more than I expected. I thought I'd read a novel or two, feel lonely and sorry for myself, botch up closing the cabin and go home miserable.''

His eyes sparkled in the firelight. ''I messed up the book-reading, didn't I?''

''You did, but you saved me from the other consequences.''

''I'm glad.''

Darkness had lowered, and Tess tilted her head back to gaze into the star-spangled sky. Away from the city lights, the Milky Way spread above them across the ebony universe. She smiled into the darkness. ''Look at the sky.''

Ryan focused upward at the brilliant display. ''Like fireworks.''

They sat in near silence with only the measured rush of the waves lapping against the shore and the crackle of the fire.

''Listen,'' Tess whispered.

Ryan sat unmoving beside her. The silence stretched to minutes. ''Nothing.''

''I know. You'll never hear silence like this in Birmingham or Rochester.''

''You can say that again.''

His earlier playfulness traveled through her mind, and she looked at him, her mouth ready to repeat her sentence. But instead of silliness, Ryan brushed her chin, then drew his fingers to the nape of her neck. A tingle shivered down her arms, leaving her breathless and wanting more.

Tess captured his strong jaw between her palms,

feeling the evening stubble of his whiskers and breathing in the heady aroma that surrounded him.

He drew her closer, tilting his chair toward her, his look caressing her face as completely as his fingers had done. "I'm trying to behave myself."

"You are," she agreed, wishing against good sense he hadn't stopped.

As he released her, his tilted chair toppled sideways. Thrashing his arms, he flipped into the sand.

A barrage of laughter split the quiet night, and Ryan jumped up, nearly hopping into the glowing embers before he regained his balance. As he brushed at his clothing, his voice echoed his embarrassment. "Now that was silly."

Tess swallowed her laughter. "But cute."

"Cute for you, not me. I'm covered in sand."

"Help me up, and I'll brush you off."

She stretched her hands toward him, and he pulled her from the chair. She brushed the back of his jacket as he dusted the front.

When they cleaned him off as best they could, Tess took his hands in hers. "If I say something, please don't laugh."

He peered at her in the firelight. "Laugh? Why would I?"

"Because I'll sound sappy."

"And?" A wry grin flickered on his face.

"I deserved that. Anyway, I'm serious now." She pressed her fingers to his lips as he had done once to her. "I have to be honest with you. I feel as if, well, as if our meeting was sort of arranged. Like this was meant to be. Do you know what I mean?" From the expression on his face, she knew he had.

"Tess, I've felt it since I saw you behind the cabin. To be honest, years earlier I wished you'd been single. I thought you were a wonderful woman, and I wished I would have met you first...but you were married and I respected that."

Her heart soared. "I've never felt so wonderful in years."

He slid his arms around her shoulder, and she moved into his embrace as if she had always belonged there.

"And it's not as if we're total strangers," she added, reliving the feeling she'd had since they met.

"We're like old friends." He tilted her face to his. "Well, not so old, and maybe, more than friends."

Lifting her lips to his, they kissed, kindling a flame stronger than the one that warmed them earlier. Ryan eased back and kissed the end of her nose. "I suppose we should put out the fire." His chuckle punctuated his double meaning.

Ryan spread sand on the embers and gathered the chairs. Tess carried the flashlight and guided them toward the cottage glowing warmly at the top of the rise. Their free hands joined in the darkness, and she felt safe and loved.

"How about some hot chocolate before I walk you back? We need to talk about tomorrow anyway."

"Sounds good. I packed as much as I could before we went to dinner. You can help me with the rest in the morning."

They entered Jill's cottage, and Ryan put on the kettle. "Relax. This'll be ready in a few minutes."

Tess plopped into an easy chair, enjoying her view of Ryan working in the kitchen. As he filled the cups, she grinned when he added some tiny marshmallows.

"Marshmallows? You planned ahead."

"The only way to drink hot chocolate." Then he confessed, "Jill must have them here for Davie."

Ryan gazed at Tess's warm smile. Things seemed perfect. He carried the mug to her side and settled in a chair. How could a few days change his life so completely? Their gazes met, and contentment washed over him.

The dim lamplight played on her wavy dark hair, her translucent skin in the soft glow, and her electric blue eyes. She was beautiful and fragile, inside and out.

"Why are you so quiet?" She raised the mug and blew on her hot drink.

"Thinking about you. I don't want to overwhelm you with a list of your wonderful attributes."

A soft flush rose to her cheeks. "Try me."

He loved the way her eyes brightened and color rose on her face. "I'll keep you dangling. Maybe you'll want to see me again when we get back home so you can hear the list I came up with."

"Oh, really."

Her leaving tomorrow had set his emotions on edge. Ryan wanted to see her again, to spend time together like they had these few days. Donna's call seemed a minor problem. Once he talked with her, she'd realize they had made the right decision.

A deep urge settled in his chest. An urge to be honest and tell Tess that he and Donna had only ended their engagement a few weeks earlier. Tell her that Donna had called today, but that he had no intention of getting back with her. His only dream was to get to know Tess better and someday...

As Ryan basked in his warm thoughts, a sound struck his ear. He jumped, the cocoa sloshing from the mug to his jeans.

"What was that?" Tess asked, staring toward the door.

"An animal...maybe," he said, yet knowing full well he'd heard a car door slam.

This time a clear knock penetrated the silence. Ryan looked at Tess, then the door. No one would come to the cabin except for an emergency. He dashed toward it while Tess sat clinging to the edge of her chair.

His heart plummeted to the ground when he saw the intruder.

Donna.

Chapter Eight

Perspiration beaded Ryan's hairline as he stared at Donna. "What are you doing here?"

"I thought you'd be happy to see me," she said in the doorway as she draped her arms around his neck in greeting. Embarrassed, Ryan quickly disentangled himself from her embrace. She stepped over the threshold and came to a dead stop, her smile skewing to a glower. "But I didn't know you had company?"

In panic, Ryan turned to Tess, seeing his worst nightmare coming to fruition. "Tess, I hadn't any—"

Tess rose, her face frozen in shock and dismay. She grabbed her jacket from the chair.

"Please, let me explain." He stepped toward her pleading for her to stay. But in a heartbeat, she slipped past Donna out the door.

Ryan gaped at her, a sense of foreboding thundering through his body. "I have a problem here, Donna." Ryan didn't care anymore. He grabbed a flashlight from a nearby doorsill, brushed past her and dashed from the cottage into the black night following Tess. He took a shortcut through the woods, branches tearing his sleeves, ruts tripping his steps as he called to her. "Tess, please wait. Please. Let me explain."

He heard the snap of twigs and the rustle of underbrush ahead of him, but in the pitch-black, she had gotten too far. When he came to the clearing, she was already inside the cabin.

Ryan tried the door, but she'd thrown on the lock and he pounded against the heavy wood. "Tess, please. Talk to me."

He darted around the cabin, pressing his face against the windows like a Peeping Tom, but she proceeded him, snapping off the lights one step ahead of him.

"I'll sit here all night, Tess. Let me talk to you. I can explain." His voice knotted, choking his words. He leaned his head against the bedroom window where the last light had been extinguished. "Open the window so you can hear me, Tess. Use a little reason."

The cabin lay in silence.

Use a little reason. Why hadn't he heeded his own words? He'd been stupid. Why hadn't he told her Donna had called? That would have been simple. Surely she would have understood. Now he had done more damage than he could ever imagine.

He stared at the dark cabin, his lone light, one pitiful ray piercing the gloom. It was as pitiful as the empty hope that lit his darkened heart.

Sitting outside in the cold woods was senseless. He had to talk with Donna and send her to a motel for the night. No need explaining anything to Donna now. At this point, after what she'd seen, he figured things were clear.

He turned away from the cabin. No matter how irritated he was with Donna, he'd never wanted to hurt her. He would send her on her way, and come back to Tess's early in the morning. Maybe she'd listen to his explanation then. A night's sleep might help them both.

Tess listened to Ryan pounding on the door, curled on top of the bed with a quilt tossed over her head. By the time the cabin had grown silent, her tears had dried. How could she have believed him? He'd joked that all men lie. That he didn't lie. Apparently that had been another deception.

Earlier she had fought herself not to open the door. She wanted to hear his explanation…even in front of Donna. She longed for a thread of reason. Anything to make the hurt go away and bring back the contentment she'd felt only minutes earlier. But she found no reason. Only more dishonesty.

Now in silence, she rose on tiptoe and crept through the cabin, peeking through the windows. Finally, she decided that Ryan had gone back to the cottage. Spurred by her need to get away, Tess did her best to pack on her own and not wait until morning. She would leave tonight.

Having given Ryan her address and telephone number, Tess suspected he'd call. But she wouldn't answer. She wouldn't listen. She had no judgment to tell truth from lies.

Tess's head pounded as she thought about his business card. She wanted to destroy it, but some deep hope clung to her heart—a small thread of faith. Could the warm, loving feelings have been totally wrong? She thought back to her life with Al. Though she didn't see the truth, she wasn't ignorant. She sensed things weren't right. In truth, she hadn't wanted to know. She'd deluded herself. Had she done that again, wanting so badly to feel loved and desired? Her question swung from despair to hope.

In the darkness and her inexperience, Tess turned off the water, leaving the taps open just enough so the wrapped pipes wouldn't burst. She remembered Al doing that. She prayed she had done the job correctly. She reviewed the list of tasks to close the cabin for the winter. With haste, she threw her luggage and storage boxes into the car.

Pulling the shutters closed, she secured them inside, then pulled the fuses from the box. Locking the door, she climbed into the car. Tears rolled down her cheeks and dripped from her chin as she dug in her jacket pocket for her keys. Along with her keys, she felt something else. She dug them out and gazed at the smooth pink heart-shaped stone Ryan had given her. Tempted to toss it out the window, she closed her hand around the rock and slid it back into her pocket, then pulled down the rutted lane to the dark highway and headed home.

Since leaving Mackinaw City, Ryan hadn't been the same. That night, Donna had been furious and tore away from the place as if he'd cheated on her…and perhaps he had. He should have talked with her on the telephone and made things right then. His head swirled with "what ifs." All he knew was that love had found him that night in the woods and he wasn't going to let a misunderstanding ruin his chances to love the way God meant him to love.

The next morning, he'd gone to Tess's cabin and found the shutters locked, everything secured and Tess already gone. His heart felt weighted with loss and loneliness. He closed Jill's cottage and left the northern city, his emotions as raw and aching as if someone he loved had died.

For the past two weeks, he'd dialed Tess's phone number time after time, but the answering machine always picked up, and Tess never returned his call. No matter what he did or said to make things better, how could he right the wrong he'd done?

He imagined how hurt Tess had been, opening her heart to him, speaking of trust, and in the next hour, he had let her be hurt by Donna's surprise visit. He could blame Donna, but he knew where the blame lay. He grimaced, thinking how similar it seemed to Tess's husband's dreadful surprise.

With frustration charging through him, Ryan left

the office and headed for his sister's house. Jill could give him some needed guidance through a woman's eyes. Gary had just gotten back to work following his appendectomy and with Davie in kindergarten, Ryan hoped Jill would be home alone. He needed to talk.

When she opened the door, her knowing gaze smacked him with the truth. "You look terrible. What's wrong?"

Ryan mumbled about his northern romance and the horrible story of Donna's unexpected appearance.

Jill's eyes rolled throughout his narration, and her sputtered comments seemed less than helpful.

Finally, he fell back against the sofa cushion and closed his mouth. He'd apologized to Tess with the same comment, "Open mouth, insert foot," and he felt as if he'd done that today with Jill.

"I'm sorry, Ryan. I guess I don't seem sympathetic, but you were an absolute fool. I don't understand how you got yourself into this mess. You're an honest guy. You're a gentleman…in every sense of the word. So explain."

"I don't know, Jill. One thing led to another. I was the kind stranger who helped her out of a couple of problems. We talked, and it felt nice to have another person nearby. I offered to help her close up the cabin. She seemed lonely and a little pensive. I started out as Mr. Macho. You know, 'Here he comes to save the day.' The next thing I know, I invited her to the island. There was a gorgeous sunset. She bought a sweatshirt and I used the clothes hanger to get into my car, and—''

"Wait a minute. I followed you until the hanger."

Ryan recounted the twin stories of the locked keys. "Somehow, in that moment, I kissed her…and she kissed me back. In my gut, she seemed like an old friend, a fellow traveler in the world of problems and laughter. We were like two lost souls finding each other."

"You've been reading too many women's magazines." Jill shook her head. "Why weren't you upfront? Why not tell her your breakup was fresh, but the feelings had died long before. Why didn't you tell her that Donna called, but you weren't going to change your mind?"

Ryan's heart sank. What Jill said sounded so easy. "I didn't want to add tension to an already-edgy situation."

"I don't blame her for leaving when she saw Donna. Not one bit. If I'd trusted a man, let him kiss me, listened to his poetic rambling about lost souls and fellow travelers, I'd have run out on you, too, when another woman showed up."

"I'd planned to tell her…after the fact."

Jill rubbed her neck. "But you forgot to tell your plan to Donna. If you had, she wouldn't have shown up."

He grimaced. "Right. So now I need a plan of action."

"That's the first thing you've said that makes sense. But I'm wondering if you're too late, Ryan. I don't know Tess well, but I understand how badly she was hurt. The summer after her husband's death, we sat on the beach for a long time and she poured out her heart. She wondered if she could ever trust again. She asked me about Gary. Why did I trust him? Did I ever suspect that he was cheating on me? How did I make him satisfied and happy? She sounded as if she felt guilty for some reason.''

As he listened to Jill's description, Ryan slumped deeper into the cushion, wishing he could vanish. He'd seen Tess's vulnerability. He'd heard her remarks about commitment and promises. Why hadn't he been open then and not taken chances?

''Sitting there with a hangdog face isn't helping, Ryan. The poor woman was blaming herself. It sounds like after two years she finally found the courage to trust someone—and you really threw her a curve.''

''I know.''

''So do something to prove how much Tess means to you. But there are no guarantees.''

No guarantees. Jill was right. But he had to take a chance. He and Tess had been soul mates, sharing thoughts and feelings. She was meant for him—the hand of God had moved the earth. He had no doubt. Somehow he had to convince her he cared about her more than words could say.

Tess closed her front door and gazed at the wrapped floral bouquet. She carried it to the end table by the window and detached the small card. Ryan.

Tears blurred in her eyes as she looked at his signature and simple message. "Please talk with me."

She crumpled into a nearby chair while her thoughts drifted back to Mackinaw. Images of their footprints in the sand rose in her memory, imprints washed away by the tide just like Ryan had torn away a piece of her heart. Old beliefs charged through her head. *Emotions are fleeting. Love is devious. Men are fickle and dishonest.*

Tess's thoughts shot back to her life with Al. He brought her flowers on occasion, often after one of his extralong weekends or his very, very late evenings at the office. Were these flowers like Al's—to salve Ryan's guilt? Or could she be totally wrong? Were they a reminder of their hours on the island and their first kiss?

She brushed unbidden tears from her lashes and grabbed the telephone. She'd told no one about the incident with Ryan, and today the memory weighed on her like a boulder.

Tess dialed her brother's telephone number. Maybe Dan wouldn't understand, but Helen might offer her a sympathetic ear.

After their hellos, Helen's comment was direct. "So what happened up north? I wondered why we hadn't heard from you lately.

Tess's emotions bubbled to the surface. "I can't talk about it…or I'll cry."

"Tell me, Tess. I'm not just your sister-in-law. I'm your friend."

Pleased that Helen seemed so ready to listen, Tess

emptied her confusion onto the table like a puzzle and sorted the pieces. She began with their humorous meeting in the woods, the firelight, the island, the sunsets and finally, to Donna's arrival.

"You're kidding. The rat." Helen spit her sentiment into the air. "He doesn't deserve a woman like you. You're better off without him."

But Tess's tears had won out and Helen's voice softened. "He really took a slice of your heart, didn't he? I'm sorry."

"You'd understand if you'd been with him. He seemed so...gentle and honest. We shared our feelings and thoughts. And his eyes were—"

Helen gasped. "Tess, you didn't—"

"No. Absolutely not. I'm not that stupid. But I wanted to, Helen. For the first time since long before Al died, I yearned to be in his arms, to be loved by someone that tender and kind."

"Tess, you're not naive. You read people well. Could you be wrong? He might have a reasonable explanation. Did you ask? Did you let him explain?"

"I ran off that night and left. Drove away before morning, and I haven't answered his calls." Emotion thundered through her, and Tess pressed her hand against her aching chest. Could Helen be right? Could there be some plausible justification? No, how could there be? She saw Donna. She saw Ryan. "Now he's sent me flowers."

"You could be wrong, Tess."

"I don't think so."

Helen's sigh shivered through the wire. "Think about it, Tess. Do you have his phone number?"

"Yes. I have his business card. He's in real estate, and I asked him to do an appraisal on the cabin."

"An appraisal?" Helen said with question. "Maybe you should call him. Give him a chance to explain."

"I was probably a fling. That's all."

"Remember, Ryan isn't Al, Tess. Ask God for help. Have you forgotten about prayer?"

Chapter Nine

Ryan sat at his desk, staring at Tess's market evaluation. He missed her more than he could imagine. He'd wrestled with his thoughts. Was their relationship like the shipboard romance that he and Tess had joked about? He believed not.

In their lengthy conversations, they'd talked about hopes, dreams, beliefs, and they'd laughed at each other and themselves. He meant what he'd said about God's direction. Some things were meant to be. And in his heart, he sensed they were part of the big picture, the scheme of things.

He'd called Tess so many times, longing to hear her voice when all he heard was the answering machine. He thought about the couple who'd dropped by the office, interested in purchasing northern property. When he told them about Tess's cabin, they were anxious to look at it. Was this God's hand? Would Tess return his call for a possible sale?

In truth, he hated to see her sell the cabin. She loved it so much. The property offered a prime view of the island and bridge. She'd never find an excellent parcel of land like that again.

Besides, he'd told her to wait through the winter to make a decision. If he phoned, it would be putting pressure on her. Even if he did, would she speak to him? No matter, he couldn't bear waiting much longer without hearing her voice.

Looking at the clock, he calculated she would be home from her school job. He picked up the phone and punched in her number. After three rings, he pulled the receiver from his ear ready to hang up, but at that moment, he heard her voice.

His heart lurched. "Tess, this is Ryan. Please don't hang up."

Silence hung heavy between them.

"Thank you for the flowers," she whispered finally. "What do you want, Ryan?"

Her cold voice sent icy waves through his chest. He wanted to tell her the truth. *I want you, Tess. I want you to understand what happened.* But he couldn't. He had to ease into it. Move slowly.

"I wanted you to know…I had the cabin assessed. And I, uh, I might have a buyer if you're still interested in selling."

He waited, and the silence wrapped around his heart as heavy as it hung on the air. "Are you there, Tess?"

"Yes. I'm thinking."

Her voice sounded aloof and deliberate. Her reserve rose between them like a stone wall, and all he could answer was a pitiful "Oh." He waited, the open telephone line humming with emptiness, except her breathing.

"Yes. I want to get rid of it," she said finally.

"You do?" With disappointment, her words slithered through him.

"Too many memories." Her hesitation weighted the air.

Ryan drew in a deep, hopeful breath. "I'll need to meet with you then to get your signature."

"I'm really busy, Ryan."

Her words punched him in the solar plexus. "I could drop by...tomorrow night." He held his breath.

"All right. I suppose that'll work." She sighed. "I need to get my furniture and things out of—"

"Tess, don't worry about that now. First, I'll see if they're even interested."

"Okay."

"I'll see you tomorrow, then."

He listened to the silence, wondering what more he could say. "I guess that's it."

She hung up abruptly, and Ryan forced down the knot of emotion lodged in his throat. He'd never felt so alone.

Tess stared at the listing agreement and felt tears push at the back of her eyes. She didn't want to cry. Not in front of anyone and especially not in front of Ryan.

"Just sign here," Ryan said, pointing to the line. "But if you're not sure—"

"I'm sure," she said, swallowing her emotion. She scrawled her name and dropped the pen.

Ryan closed the ballpoint and slid it into his pocket, then slipped the paper into his attaché case, but instead of rising, he sat and looked at her.

"Tess, I don't know why you're doing this. I realize I told you I might have a buyer, but I can see in your face you're not ready to make this decision. I can tear up the agreement."

His words washed toward her like a lifesaver—but she pushed them away, preferring to drown in her self-pity. "I'm fine with it, Ryan. I'm sure I'll be relieved once it's over. It's just the place was always—"

"Your sanctuary. The place you draw in the breath of life. Your autumn that gives you hope for a new spring. I know. We talked about it."

"We did," she said, letting the memories swarm into her mind like bees, stinging her awareness.

"I don't mean to hurt you any more than I have. All I mean is…all I want you to know is I used this as an excuse to talk with you. I—"

"You mean you deceived me again?" She peered at him, disbelieving.

"No. I didn't lie about the buyers. That's true, but I could have waited and not rushed this. I just wanted a chance to talk with you." He lowered his head and stared at the tabletop. "To explain what happened."

Explain what happened? She'd seen what happened, yet Tess hadn't allowed him to explain. Her heart felt a gentle nudge of compassion as if God were reminding her how a Christian should act. Do not judge. Do not take the beam from someone's eye until you remove the mote from your own. Did she have a speck in her eye? She drew in a deep breath. Perhaps she did.

"Tell me now, Ryan. I'll listen."

"Let's go to dinner, Tess. Let me take you out and we can talk there." His face looked desperate.

Her heart softened. "You mean in a neutral corner." Despite her attempt to remain serious, she felt a faint grin curve her lips.

Two days later, Tess carried dishes from her brother's dining room table into the kitchen. Helen stood loading them into the dishwasher.

Dan came through the doorway with another stack and set them in the sink. "I think I'll let you ladies talk while I go watch the football game. What do you say?"

"What's new?" Helen said, flashing him a grin. "Just keep the kids happy."

Tess grinned, watching their comfortable banter. She enjoyed Sunday dinners at her brother's house, and she loved seeing her young nieces.

Dan filled his coffee cup and left the room while Tess headed for the sink to rinse the dishes. Since the dinner with Ryan, her mind was heavy with thought. He'd explained and she accepted his answer.

She'd been too quick to jump. Too fearful from the past baggage she dragged around with her.

Just like Helen had reminded her earlier, Ryan wasn't Al. That was true, but as soon as her heart eased, another fact ballooned above her. Ryan should be a family man. A man with a wife and children. Tess had miscarried twice. How was she to know if she could ever carry a child? She'd never had another chance.

The reality seared through her like a branding iron. She'd lived with that fear since Al's death.

"So you saw him," Helen said from behind Tess.

She jumped at the sound. "Yes. We had dinner. It was nice."

"You've forgiven him, then?"

"I admitted I'd jumped to conclusions too quickly. I hadn't given him a chance to explain, but at that time, I couldn't concoct anything that made sense. You have to realize I trusted Al. He was my husband. I'd trusted him with all my heart. Can you imagine how the deception hurt? How it destroyed my faith in people? My trust?"

Helen clutched Tess's shoulder and shook her head. "I'd be lying to say I did, but everyone doesn't act like Al. Look at Dan. I have no question he's been faithful. Not all men run around, Tess. I just hope you give Ryan a chance."

Her wish slithered through Tess's thoughts. "I've said I'm sorry, but I... I don't know. I just don't think I have a future...with anyone."

"Why not? You have a lifetime, Tess. You seem

to like Ryan a lot and you like his family. The two of you only had a few days together. You have a lifetime to give him—or someone—a chance.''

A lifetime. A lifetime without children, perhaps. It wasn't fair.

"We'll see," Tess said, knowing she'd already decided. "Anyway, I know I need change in my life. I've been thinking about selling the house."

Helen gave her a questioning stare. "Your house?"

"Maybe I'll buy a condo. No yard work. No outside building maintenance. Perfect for a single woman." She handed Helen the last dish.

Helen slipped it into the dishwasher and closed the door, then turned and rested her back against it. "I think you should take time to decide that, too, Tess. Really. You've decided to sell the cabin. Now your house. You can't run away from life. You can't close doors on everything."

Was that what she was doing? Tess shrugged. "I don't know. I feel I need to do something."

Helen shook her head. "I think you could do something less drastic than selling your home. For one, you could give Ryan a chance."

Ryan gazed outside at the Open House sign stuck into the lawn. He hated these long Sundays, waiting for prospective buyers to drop by. Today he'd taken only two families through the condo.

He glanced at his watch. One more hour. He released a sigh and propped his elbows on the kitchen table to hold up his chin, then listened for the front door to open.

Since the night he'd had dinner with Tess, sleep had escaped him. They'd had a good talk. Even a few laughs, but Tess didn't budge. Even though she said she believed him and understood what happened, she didn't want to see him. She said they had nothing to offer each other.

The words smacked his heart a second time. How could she say it? They had so much to offer each other. They'd spent days together sharing the things they enjoyed—and enjoying the things they shared. Her attitude made no sense.

A sound from outside caught Ryan's attention. Someone came through the front door, and he rose and strode to greet the new client.

Passing through the archway, he halted. "Tess."

"Ryan."

"What are you doing here?"

"Looking for a condo."

"A condo? You never mentioned wanting a new place."

She shrugged. "I'm making changes, I guess."

The autumn sun streamed through the wide front window and shot red highlights through her hair. She stepped forward, averting her gaze, and pivoted as she eyed the room.

"Let me show you around," Ryan said, keeping his voice from reflecting his unwieldy emotion.

She followed, and he pointed out the main features

as his mind scrambled with some way to set things right between them.

"I don't know," she said, standing in the kitchen. "I suppose I'm spoiled, living in a house. I never thought about sharing walls with other families."

Ryan drew in a lengthy breath. "I have stand-alone condos I can show you, Tess, but please, have a seat." He gestured to the kitchen table. "I'll show you some other listings."

She waited while Ryan pulled a chair beside hers, then lifted a bound listing book from his case and laid it in front of her. "Why are you giving up your house, Tess?"

She shrugged and turned the pages to face her. "I need change."

"But you're selling the cabin. Isn't that enough?"

She shrugged a shoulder.

"I'm taking the buyer up to Mackinaw this week. You sure want me to do that?"

She nodded.

"You can come along, and I'll get you home before Thanksgiving."

"No, you go ahead."

Sending up a quick prayer, Ryan slid his hand over hers. "Let me give you a change, Tess. Not a house, but me. A friend. A chance to get to know each other. No permanent commitment…now. Just a faithful, honest friendship."

She didn't draw away her hand. Instead she gazed at him with moisture pooling against her lashes. "I miss you, Ryan."

His heart leaped, and he cradled her hand deeper into his. "I miss you. I know we don't know each other well, as time goes, but I feel in my heart I've known you forever."

She nodded, her voice a whisper. "Me, too."

"What do you say?" He rose and drew her to his side. "Good friends? Companions in this lonely world?" He grinned, thinking of Jill's comment that he'd read too many women's magazines.

Tess smiled, too, for her own reasons. "Friends only. Okay?"

He nodded, hoping one day she'd change her mind. Then he drew her up to stand beside him, and with gazes riveted, as if each were seeking answers from the soul, Ryan slipped his arm around Tess's shoulder and drew her closer. She didn't resist, but rested her body against his, a slight tremor rippling through her.

He tilted his head to see her face, her lips moist and soft-looking in the sunlight that streamed through the window. Without restraint, he lowered his mouth to hers, and Tess accepted it, yielded to it as if time had stood still, and they were again standing in the woods, watching leaves flutter to the ground and hearing waves roll to the shore.

"To friendship," he said when he eased his lips from hers.

"Friendship," she whispered.

Chapter Ten

Tess lowered her legs from the bed and walked to the window, looking down on her parents' driveway. She'd decided to take a couple extra days and come early for the holiday. To Tess, the little town of Holly seemed the only place to be for Thanksgiving—her parents, her childhood home, her family church and her youth.

The town suffused her in memories: hayrides, skating on the winter ponds, walks in the spring rain, swimming in the lakes nearby. A life that had seemed endless and perfect. But now she realized life wasn't always perfect.

Since she'd had the talk with Ryan a few days earlier, she'd tried to relax and enjoy his company, but she found herself struggling with so many things. Most important, she cared about him too much.

She'd been the one to insist on friendship only…and for her own purpose. Ryan should have a wife and children. Children she might not have—or children that she might miscarry, sending her husband, discouraged, to another woman's arms. A fertile woman who could give him children.

Tess had accepted the blame. But she couldn't do it again. She couldn't put Ryan through that. She had to rein in her emotions while wondering if her first decision had been the best—the decision not to see him at all.

She wiped the condensation from the window as she thought about Ryan in Mackinaw. The idea of selling her northern property weighed deeply on her heart despite what she'd told him.

Taking her time, Tess showered and dressed, then ambled downstairs for breakfast. She couldn't hide much from her parents so she expected to be grilled as thoroughly as the morning's breakfast sausage she'd smelled drifting beneath her doorway.

Tess reached the landing, plastered a smile on her face and walked into the kitchen.

Ryan's car faltered, then picked up speed again. Puzzled, he checked the gauges on the console. Something was wrong. This had probably been a bad time to travel up north for an overnight trip to show Tess's cabin with the Thanksgiving holiday this week, but the couple had liked the idea. He'd looked forward to seeing the cabin again, to recall the warm feelings he'd shared with Tess. But instead, he encountered a lonely, forlorn feeling.

Now as he was returning home, traffic on the freeway was heavy with travelers heading places for the Thanksgiving holiday. Years ago, motorists would stop to help, but today, people were cautious. If something was wrong with his car, he had no desire to be stranded on the freeway.

The motor faltered again, and Ryan eyed the exit signs. He'd already passed Flint so he wasn't too far from home. Holly was the next exit. Maybe he could take the back roads home. At least, he'd be nearer a service station.

The city of Holly rang a bell, and Ryan searched his memory. Tess's family lived in Holly, he recalled and she'd mentioned being in town for the holiday. The recollection sent gooseflesh down his arms. Could this be God's hand, again, guiding him up the freeway exit ramp?

He followed the sign and drove the few miles away from the freeway into town. It was busier…and stranger than he expected. Women ambled along the sidewalks in long dresses and bonnets, covered in winter wraps with fur collars. Men with top hats and frock coats headed into stores, seemingly filled with customers. Dressed in knickers and caps, little boys played along the side streets barricaded to traffic.

From his memory flew the answer. The Dickens Celebration. Thanksgiving was the opening of the Christmas Carol pageant with Tiny Tim and Ebenezer Scrooge, played on the streets of Holly. He'd never seen the festivities, but others had told him.

In the center of town, Ryan eyed a service station.

Feeling the car faltering again, he headed toward it, passing a man selling roasted chestnuts. The little town took him back in time, and at this moment, he wished he had a horse, instead of his dying automobile.

Frustrated, Ryan parked along the service station fence and headed inside. He checked his watch. Almost noon. How long would he be stranded here? His stomach rumbled, and his neck ached from the drive and from the stress-filled situation.

Ryan's wait was short, and when he told the mechanic the problem, the man lifted his hood and, without delay, pointed to the difficulty. His drive belt had frayed and was holding only by a thread.

"So how long?" Ryan asked. "I'm traveling."

"Not in this car, you aren't." The young fellow gave him a toothy grin. "At least, not 'til we replace this belt."

"I know," Ryan said, trying to offer him a pleasant look. "But how long to fix it?"

"Shouldn't take more than an hour," the fellow said, his smile broadening.

"Great." Ryan's anxiety faded. "I'll get some lunch and come back."

The man chuckled. "Hold on there. About an hour…when we get a drive belt."

Ryan wasn't in the mood for the man's joviality. "You don't have one in stock?"

"Nope. I'll run in and see when we can get it. Have to order one from the dealer." He held up a finger and headed back inside.

The nippy air sent a chill down Ryan's back. Or was it disappointment? He released a heavy sigh and followed the mechanic. If not one hour, then how many?

Ryan watched the man's face as he spoke on the phone, feeling his heart slip to his boots. He picked up words. *Thanksgiving. Friday.* Today was Wednesday. He was supposed to be in the office today. Who could he call to drive him home? Then he'd have to get a ride back to pick up his car.

Or he'd rent a car. Scanning the main street, his hopes drooped. The town seemed too small for a car rental. Forget the office. Why hurry back anyway? Nothing waited for him there. But here, something did…if he had any idea where Tess's family lived. Even their last name.

Given the bad news, Ryan pondered his next move. The mechanic mentioned a motel within walking distance. He decided to leave his bag in the car until he had a room. With his luck, Ryan figured the motel would probably be booked for the Thanksgiving holiday.

He stuffed his hands into his jacket pocket and headed in the direction of the motel. Tempting aromas drifted from storefronts: spicy apples, fresh baked bread and plain old hamburgers. His stomach growled again, reminding him he hadn't eaten for hours. Motel first, then food.

And if he only knew Tess's maiden name. He'd

never yearned so badly for a friendly face. Her lovely smile. If he ever needed God working in his favor, the time was now.

Tess bundled into her warmest clothing and headed downstairs to join the family for their holiday tradition—the Dickens's skit outside the Holly Hotel and then lunch in the historic building, famous for its resident ghost and vivid history.

"I'll drive," Tess offered as the family headed outside. "I'm blocking Daddy's car."

"You women always lollygag in those shops. How about we take two cars?" her dad suggested.

"Clarence, be nice," Rose said. "How often does Tess come for a visit?"

Tess chuckled at her mother's unnecessary concern and opened her car door. "Anyone want to ride with me?"

"Sure," Dan said, then called to their folks. "Helen and I'll ride with Tess. Will you take the kids?"

He grinned when they hollered sure. Dan and Helen climbed into her car. As Tess pulled out of the driveway, she turned on the radio, hoping to discourage any more probing questions from her brother about Ryan. To her relief, everyday conversation filled the few minutes to town.

After parking, the family reunited and wandered toward the hotel, passing the holiday-decked shops that lined the street and filled the old buildings.

Outside the hotel, crowds had gathered to watch the presentation of Dickens's *Christmas Carol.* Tess and her family huddled together on the sidewalk awaiting the appearance of Tiny Tim and Ebenezer Scrooge.

But before the play began, a strange sensation prickled at the nape of Tess's neck like a feather grazing her skin. She raised her hand and brushed away the feeling. The tingle rippled down her arms, sending a chill to the marrow of her bones.

Curious, she pivoted her head as best she could without turning around. Her heart soared. Ryan stood in the midst of the nearby crowd.

Why was he here in Holly? She searched her memory. She'd never mentioned where her parents lived. Or had she? Vaguely she recalled telling him she'd grown up here. But had he expected to find her here? Before she made her way through the crowd, Ryan's gaze found hers.

His expression duplicated her own astonishment. She waved and watched him maneuver through the crowd.

When he slipped beside her, Tess lifted her hand to calm her pounding heart. Looking at him with a multitude of questions surfacing, the sun brightened, sending an unexpected warmth penetrating her heavy coat.

''What are you doing here?'' she whispered. His smile warmed her more than the sun.

The crowd had begun to hush, and he gestured toward the players ready to begin. ''It's a long story. I'll tell you later.''

Tess harnessed her questions while Ryan grasped

her hand and gave it a gentle squeeze. They didn't speak, and Tess agreed there was no need.

Her mother glanced their way and arched an eyebrow. Tess lifted her finger to her lips, hoping she'd be patient and wait for the explanation.

Sensing her brother's probing look, Tess shifted her gaze to Dan whose mouth formed the word *Ryan.* Tess gave a nod and chuckled as Dan whispered the news in Helen's ear. Her nieces looked with curiosity at the stranger.

Tess refocused on the players, applauding as Scrooge dealt with the ghosts of Christmas past and present as they numbered his shortcomings and sins.

While her body reacted to Ryan's unexpected nearness, her own shortcomings filtered through her mind. She needed to learn patience and to gain trust. Al's infidelity had twisted her into her own kind of Bah-humbug Scrooge.

Standing beside Tess, Ryan's thoughts soared. Why in the world had he lingered on this street and found her standing so close? He looked upward to the blue autumn sky with the sunlight filtering through the wispy clouds and said a silent thank-you. A power greater than he had arranged this. The best luck in the world couldn't have come close.

After Scrooge said his final words and Tiny Tim called out, "God bless you, everyone," the applause broke the audience's hush. Ryan turned to Tess. "I can't believe I found you."

Her face flushed, and she raised her hand to her cheek. "Me, neither...but you did."

In seconds, her parents gathered around, and they stepped off the sidewalk to avoid blocking the dispersing crowd.

Tess gestured. "Mom, Dad, this is Ryan Walsh. Ryan, my parents, Clarence and Rose Hunter."

They greeted him with smiles as friendly and warm as Tess's. She introduced Dan and Helen next, then the girls. "This is Mandy and April, my nieces."

The children grinned while Dan squeezed his arm adding a "thumbs-up." Ryan was mystified by what the gesture meant. He hoped Dan knew something he didn't.

"Who's hungry?" Clarence asked. "My stomach was nearly as loud as those actors."

"I'm sure we're all starving," Rose said. "Are you all ready? Hopefully, they'll still have a few seats for us." She gestured behind her to the hotel.

"You'll join us, Ryan?" Clarence asked.

"No, but thanks. I don't want to intrude on—"

"You're not intruding," Tess said.

Ryan chuckled. "Sounds like that answers that."

The family climbed the steep steps to the hotel lobby, now only a restaurant, and the hostess went off to arrange seating for eight.

Dan caught Ryan's arm. "Check out the bar." He gestured to the adjacent room. "Carrie Nation once stormed the place with her ax."

"The suffragette?"

"None other."

Curious, Ryan took a peek around the archway before the hostess arrived and guided them to their table. Once they had ordered, Clarence turned to him with the question Ryan assumed everyone had on their tongue. "So what brings you to Holly?"

Ryan gave a brief overview of his tale—the trip up north, his errant car, the service station and his predicament.

Tess's face still wore a puzzled expression. "I still don't understand how and why you came here?"

He shrugged. "When I decided to get off the freeway, this was the first town listed on the road sign. And here I am. Stranded."

"Glory be, if you're Tess's friend, you're not stranded anymore," Rose said. "You'll have Thanksgiving dinner with us tomorrow, naturally."

Ryan's heart stumbled, and when he looked at Tess, her eyes gave him the answer before her words.

"Mother's invited you so you'll come." She squeezed his arm. "If she hadn't, I would have suggested it."

Clarence clasped his shoulder. "Where are you staying, Ryan? You might as well pick up your things and spend the time with us, too. We can run you over to the garage Friday when your car's ready."

That was more than Ryan could hope. "No, thank you, sir. I'll manage fine. Thanksgiving dinner is more than enough."

Helen chimed in. "We won't take no. We have plenty of room."

Dan grinned at Tess. "When we're through here, go ahead and pick up Ryan's things. Helen and I can ride back to the house with Mom and Dad in the van."

"You sure?"

He gave her a wink and patted Helen's hand. Before any more was said, their food arrived.

As was the family's tradition, Tess followed her parents into the pew for the Wednesday evening Thanksgiving service, though this time was different. Ryan stood beside her as they sang the praise-filled hymns and sat beside her as they listened to the readings.

The deepest love spread through Tess. Love for her family. Her church...and her God. A God she'd closed herself from, for too long. Today her heart had opened more than ever. She'd witnessed Ryan's strong faith and his testimony helped to remind her of the Lord's grace and forgiveness.

The pastor's voice resounded through the speaker. "Do not be anxious about anything, but in everything, by prayer and petition, with thanksgiving, present your requests to God. And the peace of God, which transcends all understanding, will guard your hearts and your minds in Christ Jesus."

Tess let the words settle in her heart. *Do not be anxious about anything.* How often lately had she allowed her life to be swayed by fear and guilt?

Anxious? She'd been more than anxious about tomorrow. She'd allowed the past to burrow into her heart like worms into wood, making even the good part of her life unstable and weak.

But the pastor's words flooded her with saving grace. Make your requests known, he'd said. Pray with thanksgiving and you'll find peace.

Peace. Her gaze drifted to Ryan's strong profile, his blond hair still ruffled from the outside breeze.

Her heart soared. As if he read her mind, he turned and sent her a loving smile, so tender and sweet she wondered how she could doubt that he was the Lord's gift to her. The Lord's unexpected blessing. *All good gifts come from the Lord.* The words sailed into her mind, filling her with joy.

Ryan felt Tess's slender hand squeeze his thicker fingers, and he squeezed back. As the service progressed, her face had filled with a new peace. A peace that filled him with hope. He knew something held her back from giving her love freely. He'd wondered if it were Al's infidelity or something more. Something deeper that shrouded Tess's future with fear.

Bowing his head, Ryan lifted his concern to heaven. He opened his eyes again, flooded by the richness of his harvest. His life. Decorating the chancel were bundles of corn stalks and piles of pumpkins. Jars of jam and jelly, fruits and vegetables covered a burlap-cloaked table, reminding people that all gifts come from the Lord. Ryan thanked God for his upbringing, a mother and father who'd taught him early to praise the Lord for every blessing.

Blessings. His focus drifted to Tess, her cheeks glowing in the dim lighting. A sense of confidence washed over him. Tess loved him. He loved Tess. Time would heal all wounds.

Chapter Eleven

Tess stood outside Ryan's bedroom door. Following the service, she'd thought all evening about him—and about what God wanted her to do. She felt assured that things had happened according to the Lord's will: their meeting, running into him at the condo for sale, finding him here in Holly. Ryan could be so easy to love.

She was learning to trust again. She believed Ryan now and understood his action. Yet on occasion, old fears poked her confidence, but she shoved them away, remembering the pastor's words, ''Do not be anxious.'' God was on her side.

Thinking of Ryan brought her a smile. Tess cared about him more than she had anyone in a long time. Loved him, really, but it seemed an impossibility. They'd known each other such a little time…and she had things she hadn't had the courage to tell him. A deeper guilt. A greater fear. Before love could find a healthy hold on her heart, she had to be open. Could she do it tonight?

Tess dragged in a shivering breath and tapped on the bedroom door. Shuffling sounds came from inside, then the door opened. Dressed in sweatpants and T-shirt, Ryan peered at her. "Tess." His surprised expression brightened, and he stepped back. "Come in."

As she stepped inside, she faltered when her focus fell on the turned-down blanket and his clothes folded neatly across the chair.

He shut the door and grabbed his garments from the chair back, then motioned to her. "Sit." He dropped his things on the end of the bed.

Tess slid into the seat, wondering why she'd come.

Ryan eased onto the edge of the bed. "If I'd known I was having company, I'd have stayed dressed. Maybe even planned some refreshments. Baked a cake."

His silliness made her smile. "You're fine the way you are. I just wanted to say a couple of things."

Anxiety darkened his face, and he scowled. "Is something wrong?"

"No, I've been thinking about us."

"Me, too," he said. He slid back farther on the mattress. "Would you come here?" He patted the spot beside him. "I'll do time-out if I misbehave."

Remembering their joke, she laughed while his smile sent her heart on a gallop.

"Scout's honor," he said, crisscrossing his heart.

"You probably were never a scout." She plopped down beside him."

"I wasn't."

An unexpected laugh shot from her chest as she faced him. "So now what?"

Tess knew what. The time was perfect, and though nudged by her purpose to tell him her secret fear, she let the opportunity pass.

So now what? Ryan's heart leaped at her question and the answer that rang in his mind. Love me. He lifted his hand and traced the line of her face with his finger. "Tess, we've known each other such a short time, but if I were a betting man, I'd say we're a match made in heaven."

Her thoughtful gaze bathed him in warmth, and she pressed her palm against his cheek. "You knocked me head over heels. I think you know that."

"I hoped. I feel the same."

"But I need to think about this," she said, searching his eyes. "I need time."

Ryan captured her hand and kissed her palm. "I'll be an old man soon."

"I know, but please be patient with me."

He nodded. "You're worth the wait."

Tess paused, her face shadowed with sadness. "I'm sorry. I wish I could be more decisive. More sure of myself."

He shook his head. "I'm a patient man."

"I'm glad," she said, rising.

He captured her hand.

"I came in to ask you about the cabin. Did the couple like it?"

Looking at the longing in her eyes, Ryan wanted to tell her they hated it. But he'd promised himself to be honest. "They loved it. Willing to pay the price. I told them we'd talk after the holiday."

She lowered her eyes. "Good. I'm glad."

"Let's not talk about that now. You need to give that some more thought." With his thumb and finger, he tilted her chin upward. "Let's talk more about us."

"Us?"

He rose beside her. "No. Let's not talk." He slid his arm around her shoulder and drew her to his chest. Her eyes spoke words that tumbled through his body like somersaults. No matter what she said, she loved him. He lowered his lips to hers, praising God for his persistence.

"Snow," Tess called from her bedroom door. "It snowed overnight."

A "shush" whispered down the hallway, and Dan put a finger to his lips. "Helen's still sleeping."

"Get her up," Tess called in a stage whisper that would fill an auditorium. "Let's make a snowman."

Another door opened and two sets of sleepy eyes peeked at her. "Snowman," their voices sang out together.

"Dress warm," Tess said to the girls.

She chuckled to herself, feeling alive and excited. Dan reached her side and, playfully, covered her mouth with his hand as he edged her toward the staircase.

"It's too late," she mumbled beneath his fingers. "I woke the girls, but I have to wake Ryan."

"He's up, sis, and already had breakfast. It's almost eleven. You ladies slept in today."

"Eleven? Ryan's up already?" She eyed him from her muzzled position. "Unloose me, you scalawag. It's time everyone's up."

He laughed and dropped his hand as they reached the stairs.

Dressed in sweatpants and a shirt, Tess bounded down the steps. Anticipating the snow, she'd pulled on woolen socks found in the bottom drawer of her old dresser.

She sailed into the kitchen where everyone had gathered. Her mother stood at the kitchen counter working on a cranberry walnut salad for their dinner. The appetizing scents of turkey and stuffing already drifted in the air.

Joining the others around the table, Tess nibbled on toast washed down by steaming coffee. She felt ashamed she'd slept so late. Her mother had their Thanksgiving dinner nearly ready for an early meal.

Dan rose and set his cup in the sink. "I supposed I'd better get out there and move some of that snow."

"I'll help," Ryan said, following his lead.

"While you guys shovel, we kids can make a snowman…or I could be a good daughter and help Mom with the dinner preparations." Playfully, Tess squinted her eyes, waiting for her mother to negate her cooking suggestion.

"Nothing much to do now, Tess. You go out and play."

Everyone in the room broke into laughter, but Tess only grinned, enjoying being one of the kids and anxious to make a snowman.

Ryan rose, stretching his arms toward her, and pulled her up by her hands. Without thinking, she slid into his arms, then guardedly backed away, hoping no one noticed.

Dan rose, too, and in a clatter, the girls bounded down the stairs and into the kitchen, grabbing a piece of toast and following them out the back hall when they heard the plans.

Tess hurried behind them, and they crowded the small area, sliding on their boots and warm coats.

Outside, Ryan ran off to grab a shovel while Dan rolled out the snowblower. Tess twirled in a slow circle while the crystal flakes blanketed shrubs and trees with glinting pristine mounds.

Amazed at the depth of the overnight snowfall, Tess formed a compact sphere with the two girls, giggling beside her. They rolled the ball along the ground. Behind her, the blower sputtered and spit until a steady roar moved up and down the walkway.

They worked together, adding a second smaller sphere, then a third, and while she found sticks for arms, the girls ran around to locate things to make the face.

When the snowman was finished, she turned to

show Ryan, but before she could open her mouth, a large snowball smacked her in the shoulder, and the battle had begun.

Mandy and April joined her, laughing and chasing each other across the yard. When Ryan cornered Tess against a tree, they tumbled into the snow, breathless and wet.

"Not fair," she said.

"All's fair in love and war," he said, his breath sending white vapor into the air.

She grabbed a handful of snow and rubbed it into his face.

"Okay, you get what you deserve," Ryan said, slipping the powdery ice down her neck as he pressed his lips to hers.

Wiggling free, Tess let out a scream while Ryan jumped up and ran away chasing the girls. Watching him play with her nieces sent Tess's heart on a downhill spiral. She loved Ryan. He deserved so much. What if a child wasn't in the picture for her?

Turning, Tess caught her mother's wave in the window. In moments, everyone had put away the shovel and blower, pulled off their wet boots and coats, and followed their noses to the dining room. Though Tess felt content, seeing the Lord's bountiful gifts, confusion weighed on her heart.

"Must you leave?" Tess asked.

Ryan heard the sadness in her voice as he sat beside her in the service station parking lot. "I'd better get back to Rochester. I should go into the office today.''

''You have to?''

''I really should. I was out Wednesday, remember.''

She nodded. ''Will you call the couple? The ones who looked at the cabin.''

''No, I want you to think about your decision.''

She averted his eyes. ''I have, Ryan.''

He captured her chin and turned her face toward his, wondering if she had listened at all to what he'd said. In the past two days he told her everything but ''I love you.'' And he believed he did. No one, no other woman who'd come into his life, made him feel like Tess did.

But they needed time. She'd said it, and it was true. Right now, they could make no commitments, no promises, until they were positive that what they felt was real. He'd made the mistake once. He wouldn't make the same mistake again.

''Hang on and let me make sure the car's ready.'' He slid out of her sedan and headed inside. With a glance over his shoulder, he fixed on Tess's questioning eyes.

Inside the service station while Ryan waited for the mechanic, he glanced out the window. Tess sat with her head resting on the seat back. She was beautiful and lovable. He understood her concern. If he listened to his emotions, he'd have no question about where they were headed. But they had to use good sense. Their relationship was too fresh and new…and marriage was for a lifetime.

Turning, Ryan caught the mechanic's eye and had his question answered. His car was ready. He paid the bill and secured his car keys, then headed back to Tess.

He dangled his key chain. "It's ready."

With a nod, she shifted in the seat and rolled down the window. "I noticed."

"So when will I see you, Tess?"

She shrugged. "I guess that's up to you."

"No," he said, resting his hands on the window frame and leaning into the car. "It's up to us. You're coming home on Sunday?"

She nodded. "Probably in the afternoon."

"Then I'll call you."

She nodded, her eyes sadder than he'd ever seen. "It's been wonderful."

"It has." He chucked her under the chin. "I'll see you Sunday."

"Sunday. Drive safely. Okay? No accidents."

"I'll be fine. Tess." Her words pierced his thoughts. He kissed her lightly on the lips, then stepped back, allowing her to roll up the window. She lifted her hand in parting and pulled away.

Watching her leave, Ryan shook his head. If he'd lost his wife to another man in a fatal accident, he'd feel the same. Frightened, suspicious and unworthy. Tess needed time, and the best way he could prove his sincerity was by giving her lots of tender, loving care. He prayed he could help her see the truth.

* * *

Christmas music drifted from the speakers, and Tess shuffled through her CDs. Celebrating Thanksgiving gave her the go-ahead to pull out her holiday music. She needed the music; she needed courage to talk with Ryan, and she expected him any minute.

Hearing a noise, she went to the window, but the car sped past, and Tess reined her apprehension with a sigh. She crossed the room and sank into a chair. Her novel lay beside her with a bookmark slid between the pages. She picked up the book, then returned it to the table. As she did, she noticed the heart-shaped stone Ryan had given her. Why she'd kept it close by, she didn't know. She didn't believe in good-luck charms or talismans. Instead it had become a memento of a place she loved...a special time with the man she'd grown to care about more than she'd thought possible.

Though unhealthy apprehension still nipped at her, causing her anxious, frustrating moments, she understood the source of her problems, and with Ryan's loving ways, she had purged many of her doubts...except one. Tonight she would lay her last fear on the table.

Automobile lights reflecting in the window caught her attention. She rose, this time confident, and headed to the door. When the bell rang, she pulled it open and greeted Ryan with a tender kiss.

"I'm getting to love this," he said, slipping off his jacket.

"Love what?" she asked with a knowing look.

"Your beautiful smile and warm lips meeting me at the door."

He slipped his arm around her shoulders, and she guided him to the living room.

"I talked with the buyers," he said, giving her a squeeze.

"And?"

"The final meeting to finalize the sale is set for after Christmas. Okay?"

"That's fine," she said, feeling icy tendrils snake through her veins.

"I hope you're making the right decision, Tess." He drew her around and gazed into her eyes. "If you don't want to sign, we can—"

She shook her head, feeling tension rise up her neck.

He nestled her closer in his arms and lowered his lips to hers.

She eased away, her mind filled with purpose. "No more kisses until we talk."

A frown flashed across his face before it settled to a grin. "I can wait...if you promise." He sank onto the sofa and folded his hands.

"If you're still interested after we talk...I promise." He sat nearby on the edge of an easy chair, the word easy a paradox to her emotion.

The scowl he'd controlled earlier edged back on his face. "I'm ready," he said, though his voice had lost some of its confidence.

"Ready as you'll ever be," she said, trying to round the edges of her discomfort.

He gave her a faint smile.

Tess leaned forward, her mind working to sort out where to begin. "It seems we've talked about so much of this before, Ryan, but it's much more complicated to me than I've let you know."

Tess rubbed her fingers along her temples to control the headache she felt coming on, then took a deep breath.

"First, Ryan, I hope you know how much I care for you. You stepped out of the woods and into my life, changing my world from lonely to complete. Even when I pushed you away with my hands, my senses pulled you into my heart."

Ryan leaned forward, a look of concern growing on his face. "Don't tell me you're saying goodbye, Tess."

Chapter Twelve

Addled by his comment, Tess studied him. What had she said to make him think she wanted to say goodbye? More realistic, she wanted to say hello…by telling him the truth. The plain truth.

Tess shook her head. "No. I just need you to know where my heart has hit a road bump. A big one. I told you the story of Al's infidelity and the way it made me feel. My well-organized life fell apart. My ability to judge and to trust crumbled into dust. After Al died I began to question everything. I wasn't sure if my friends were really friends. That happens, you know, when your best friend deceives you."

"And then I messed with your head again when I wasn't honest about Donna." Ryan rose to move closer and she raised her hand to stop him.

She nodded. "Please let me finish. All that was bad enough, but now I understand it all, Ryan. I felt in my heart that I was to blame for Al's affair."

"You? I don't understand."

"I told you I'd never had children. I didn't tell you that I had a miscarriage. Not once, but twice. After it was over, Al changed. He'd wanted a family. Really looked forward to having children. The miscarriages took our excitement and hope to the pits. Can you imagine what that did to me?"

Ryan's face was twisted with sadness and sorrow filled his eyes. "I can't even guess."

"I became filled with self-pity. I wanted to be a good wife, but I felt cursed. I encouraged Al to try again, but in my heart I feared I'd never get pregnant and if I did, I'd never carry a baby to term."

"Oh, Tess," Ryan said, rising and kneeling beside her. "I'm so sorry."

"And you should be a dad, Ryan." She lifted her fingers and brushed his hair from his forehead. "You'll be such a wonderful father. I saw it with Davie and again with my nieces. You love kids. You need a wife who can give you children and a—"

Ryan captured her hand and lifted it to his lips. He kissed her fingers, her palm and wrist. "Tess. One—even two—miscarriages doesn't mean you can't have children. One confused husband doesn't mean all men make bad mates. You are the world to me, Tess. We've already agreed that God has had His hand in our relationship. He's pushed two people together in the northern woods. Two people who live near each other in lower Michigan. Two people who share the love of family and the love of the Lord. Please don't let a faint possibility ruin something that's a strong positive."

"But I wanted you to know. I wanted to be honest…finally."

"I'm relieved, Tess. Relieved and grateful that you trust me enough to tell me everything. Today we'll make a pact. Honesty always. Never hold back."

Tess nodded. "Honesty always."

"And, Tess, if we never have a child, we could adopt. Or we could be happy just being together and loving our siblings' kids. It would be what God wanted for us."

She let his words settle in her heart. Maybe she didn't totally agree, but his sincerity wrapped her in comfort.

Ryan rose and sat beside Tess. She nestled in his arms while soft carols drifted through the room. Today, Tess felt alive and whole again.

After moments of peaceful silence, Ryan shifted and lifted his hand to her cheek, then touched his lips to hers, like a feather first, before deepening the kiss, giving her the wonderful gift of trust and love. Her heart fluttered like a million butterflies. When she opened her eyes, a sweet smile glowed on his face.

"What? You're thinking something."

He nodded and slipped his hand into his jeans pocket. "I'm thinking this is the perfect time for my gift."

He withdrew a small wrapped package and placed it in her hand. Tess gazed at the small box, unable to move.

"Open it, Tess. It won't bite."

"But I… It's not—"

"Don't worry. Open it." He bent down and kissed her hair.

Her fingers trembled as she pulled the tissue from

the white box. Inside, as she suspected, she found a velvet ring box. "But I thought we—"

"Trust me." He laid his warm hand on her arm. "Trust me."

His words washed her in faith. She lifted the lid and inside found, not a diamond, but a round gold ring etched with a wreath of daisies. "It's beautiful."

"It's a friendship ring. We agreed to take our time, so I thought—"

Tears sneaked from beneath her lashes. "It's beautiful...and fitting. We are the dearest friends."

"Only friends?" he asked, his eyes teasing.

"Deep, serious, loving, nearly committed friends."

"That's more like it," he said, catching her chin with his thumb and finger.

She gazed into his loving eyes, overwhelmed by the tender sweetness. With abandon, she met his eager lips, letting her last fear drift away like an autumn leaf.

After Christmas, Tess waited in the Realtor's outer office. Today was the day. She'd put everything into Ryan's hands. All she had to do is sign the final sale papers. Not only the cabin, but its contents would be gone. It had been her decision. Keeping the furniture would only serve as a sad reminder of the place she loved so much.

In her coat, she had kept one memento. She slipped her hand inside her pocket and ran her finger over the smooth edges of the heart-shaped stone Ryan had found on the Mackinaw beach. The heart held a special meaning for her, recalling the days spent there with Ryan.

Already the emptiness filled her. She crossed her legs, and her nerves rattled with such intensity, she placed both feet on the floor to steady herself. Selling the cabin was like burying a dear friend. At times she thought about withdrawing the offer, especially now that Ryan was in her life, but she'd made an agreement and she decided to follow through no matter how much it hurt.

Sensing she was being watched, she raised her head. Ryan stood in the doorway and beckoned to her. She rose, then gathered her coat and shoulder bag. He led her down a short hall, and while she walked, she wondered about the couple who was buying the cabin. Would they love it as much as she had?

When Ryan stopped, he stepped aside and motioned her into an empty meeting room.

She stood in the doorway. "Where are the buyers? Did something happen?" Her heart wavered with a mixture of emotions. She didn't have the courage to start over again. Having the sale complete, once and for all, was easiest on her rattled nerves.

"Have a seat, Tess. Everything's fine. The sale will go on as planned."

She scowled at him, unable to understand.

He motioned to her. "Please, sit."

She sank into the chair, holding her coat and bag on her lap. "I don't understand. Where are they?"

"The buyer is right here."

"Here?"

His face flickered with emotion, and he rose and caught her hand in his. "I'm the buyer, Tess."

"You? But I don't understand."

"My dearest Tess, you don't want to sell the cabin. You love the place, and I love you. How could I sell it to strangers when I know how you feel? I told them you'd changed your mind."

Unable to find the words, she stared at him, dumb-founded.

"But…"

Before she could speak, he slipped a box into her hand.

"What is it?"

"It's for you," he said, his voice a whisper.

Her heart knew. Tearing off the lid, she gazed into the tiny box. Ignited by the sunlight from the window, the diamond shot flames of red and blue into the air. "It's beautiful, Ryan." She pressed the ring to her heart. "But I thought… You gave me this ring." She extended her friendship ring toward him.

"That's for friendship, Tess." He caught her left hand. "This ring is different. It's for love. Will you marry me, Tess? Weeks, months, years—time doesn't matter. I love you. My life won't be complete without you at my side."

Speechless, she extended her hand, and he slid the ring on her finger. Colors flickered from the ring matching the happiness shimmering in her heart. "Yes," she whispered as her lips met his.

Ryan eased away and reached across the table for the papers lying there. "Now to this other matter."

"Other matter," she said, her head swimming.

He handed her the documents. "The cabin is my wedding gift to you."

Her heart fluttered in confusion, and unable to find words, she stared at the papers.

"You're not happy?" he asked.

Her confusion melted to a smile. "I can't believe you did this for me."

He drew her into his arms, nuzzling her head against his chest.

She brushed his cheek with her finger. "Thank you. You've turned my most dreaded day into utter happiness."

He looked into her eyes. "Remember when we talked up north about autumn's promise and Thanksgiving blessings."

Tess nodded.

"This is it, Tess."

"All good gifts come from the Lord," she said.

He kissed her hair. "And you are one of my greatest gifts. I love you, Tess."

"I love you," she whispered.

Through the window, the drab December sun had brightened, and a stream of light radiated from a cloud like a promise. Home, family, love—God's gifts bound together in one man's arms, and that's exactly where she wanted to be.

Epilogue

Summer, two years later

A light August breeze blew across the water and ruffled Tess's hair. Ryan gazed at her as she plucked wisps of cotton candy from the paper cone and dropped them into her mouth.

Today their trip to Mackinac Island was leisurely. Earlier in the day, they'd taken a carriage ride around the nine-mile periphery of the island. Knowing they weren't in a hurry, they sat on the hotel porch, watching the tourists parade past, and when the last ferry of the day carried away the crowd, they rose again to amble through the quieter town.

"I like the island better now," Tess said, licking a strand of sugar candy from her lower lip.

"It's quieter. Less crowded," he said, admiring the way her skin glowed in the setting sun.

"More like our first visit here."

"It is." He caught her hand and threaded his fingers through hers. That day, nearly two years ago, filled his senses. Even then, some deep feeling had assured him that he and Tess would be together someday.

"You kissed me the next morning in the ferry parking lot. Remember?" She tilted her head to the side, nuzzling it against his shoulder.

"Remember? How could I forget that?"

Tess lifted her head slowly and peered into his eyes. "And we spent the night together...without any monkey business." Playfully, he wiggled his eyebrows.

His teasing aroused Tess's senses and she lowered her hand to feel her large rounded tummy, remembering their first night together in the cabin after the wedding.

Wrapped in joyful completeness, Tess shifted her gaze to the distant bridge and was captured by the sight, aware the Lord had granted them one more special gift. "Look, Ryan, the sunset." The colors spilled along the horizon in coral, gold and lilac, like an artist's palette, swatches of spreading color.

"Almost as pretty as you," he said, sliding his arm lower on her waist and caressing the growing child inside.

When she tugged her focus from the horizon, a familiar tourist shop came into focus. She grabbed his hand and pulled him down the street. "Ryan, look. The shop where I bought my sweatshirt."

He hurried alongside her and tugged open the

door. Inside, she wandered down the rows, browsing through the merchandise.

A salesclerk left the counter with an armful of T-shirts and hung them on a nearby rack. She smiled at Tess, then nodded to Ryan. "Is this your first overnight visit to the island?"

Ryan faltered, hearing her words.

Tess gave her a shy grin, unwilling to tell the woman the long story of her last visit to the island.

The salesclerk chuckled when she saw Tess's belly. "I thought you looked like honeymooners. Guess I was wrong."

Ryan's heart warmed at the woman's comment. Like an old song stirring warm memories, his thoughts drifted back to nearly two years earlier. Taking Tess's hand in his, he kissed her fingers and grinned at the clerk. "No. You're right...sort of. It's our second honeymoon."

Tess chuckled, and Ryan squeezed her hand, sending the Lord his deepest thanksgiving for his wife and healthy child-to-be...and for every good gift.

* * * * *

LOVING GRACE

Cynthia Rutledge

* * *

To my daughter, Wendy.
—CR

Trust in the Lord with all your heart
and lean not on your own understanding.
—*Proverbs* 3:5

Chapter One

Dr. Nicholas Tucci shrugged off his lab coat with a tired groan. Though he enjoyed the one evening a month he volunteered at the free clinic, he'd started the day with an emergency surgery at 6:00 a.m. and it was now almost midnight.

"How many patients do you think we saw tonight?" Dr. Larry Fowler collapsed on the wooden bench in front of the row of lockers that made up the doctor's lounge. "A hundred?"

"Felt like it," Nick said. "I'm sure ready for some downtime."

"Know what you're doing for Thanksgiving yet?" Larry asked, casting Nick a sideways glance.

"As a matter of fact, I've decided to go home with what's-her-name for Thanksgiving." For some reason, saying the words out loud solidified Nick's impulsive decision. "I'm in the mood for something different this year."

Actually going off for a weekend with a woman he barely knew was more crazy than different, but Nick didn't care. The way he saw it he had two choices: fight off his sister's friend all weekend or spend the holiday with a virtual stranger.

"Who are you talking about?" Larry tilted his head and stared as if Nick were speaking a foreign language.

Nick couldn't figure out why Larry was being so obtuse. After all, his friend was the one who'd told him earlier in the evening that the woman desperately needed a fill-in boyfriend for the weekend. Nick frowned and tried to recall her name. Kathy kept popping into his head but that didn't sound right. "You know very well who I mean. The redhead at the front desk."

"Grace Comstock?" Larry lifted a sandy-colored brow. "The clinic director?"

Grace. Nick smiled. The name had a classic elegance and rolled easily off his tongue.

"That's the one," Nick said. "I've decided to help her out and go home with her this weekend."

Larry laughed out loud, the sound echoing all the way to the exposed rafters. "Let me get this straight. You don't even know her name, but you're willing to pose as her boyfriend for four days?"

"I do know her name," Nick said matter-of-factly, hanging his lab coat in the locker. "It's Grace Connors."

"Comstock."

"Whatever." Nick grabbed his jacket and shut the

locker door. He fastened the combination lock and gave it a spin.

"It doesn't make sense." Larry's brows drew together in a puzzled frown. "Why would you want to spend your four days off with a stranger when you have a perfectly nice family right here in St. Louis?"

Nick had to concede that point. He did have a perfectly nice family, and Thanksgiving had always been one of his favorite holidays. Even now, thinking about his mother's turkey and stuffing, candied yams and pumpkin pie made his mouth water. And after they were all nice and full, he and his brothers would play some football before settling down in front of the tube to watch a few games.

But this year would be different. He'd known it the minute his brother Sal had told him what their sister had planned. "Because this year Raven is bringing one of her sorority sisters. She seems to think this woman would be a perfect fit for me. It's supposed to be a surprise, but my brother thought he should warn me."

"Is she in the medical field?"

"It doesn't matter." Nick raked a hand through his hair. "I don't want to date one my sister's friends."

"Why not?" Larry stared curiously at Nick. "I've seen your sister. She's gorgeous. Chances are her friend is going to be hot."

"I don't want to date anyone remotely associated with my sister," Nick repeated, more forcefully since it appeared Larry was having difficulty getting the message.

"Hmm. That is a problem." Larry thought for a moment. "I've got a radical idea. Tell her you're not interested."

Nick smiled. He supposed it did sound ridiculous...to someone who didn't know his sister. "That wouldn't stop Raven. She'd be convinced that, given time, I'd change my mind."

"But it's Thanksgiving. You don't want to be with a stranger," Larry said. "Why don't you call up Alicia or Melanie or one of the others you've dated recently? I'm sure they'd be thrilled to cook you dinner or take you home to meet Mom and Dad."

Nick could spend the next ten years explaining to Larry that it wasn't much fun dating women like Alicia, who'd already decided she loved him before she knew him, or Melanie, who'd started talking about rings after the third date. But Larry would never understand. Although Larry was a good guy, women never seemed to find him attractive.

"What can I say?" Nick shrugged. "I'm in the mood for something different. And it sounds like this woman, this Grace, is desperate."

"Not desperate enough to take you."

Nick thought he might have heard Larry wrong. But the hint of satisfaction in Larry's eyes told Nick, he'd gotten it right. "What do you mean by that?"

"She told me she doesn't like you," Larry said.

Nick raised a brow and briefly considered the thought. "That's because she doesn't know me."

Larry laughed. "I bet she says no."

"She'll agree," Nick said with a confident smile.

"Maybe so," Larry said after a long moment. "But ten bucks says you won't get so much as a single kiss from her this weekend."

Nick shook his head. Larry still didn't get it.

He wasn't looking for kisses.

All he wanted was a nice weekend with some turkey and pumpkin pie.

Nothing more.

"Do you have a minute?"

Grace Comstock's heart skipped a beat at the sound of the deep voice. She'd often thought that with such a smooth, rich baritone, Nick Tucci could have had a successful career in radio. She raised her gaze from the evening's schedule and amended her thoughts. Sticking such a man behind a microphone would have been a waste. "Dr. Nick"—as the children who visited the clinic called him—was too handsome *not* to be seen. Even now, with lines of fatigue edging his eyes and the five o'clock stubble darkening his cheeks, the sight of him made her pulse quicken.

Dressed casually in a gray sweater that accented his broad shoulders and navy pants that emphasized his lean hips, Nick looked more like a *GQ* model than a pediatric orthopedic surgeon. It was easy to see why he'd been named one of St. Louis's top ten most eligible bachelors.

Though Grace acknowledged his good looks, she

wasn't impressed. She didn't like handsome men. It had been her experience that attractive men tended to be arrogant and proud instead of praising God for the blessing of physical beauty. From what she'd seen of Nick Tucci, he fit the mold.

"What can I do for you, Doctor?" Grace used her most professional voice.

He shot her a smile and the dimple in his cheek flashed. "You can start by calling me Nick."

"O-kay." Despite her resolve to keep him at arm's length, she found herself wanting to smile back. Instead she lifted a brow. "What can I do for you, *Nick?*"

Nick hesitated, and for a moment a hint of uncertainty crept in his gaze. But then the dimple flashed in his cheek once again and he gestured to the chair next to her desk. "Mind if I sit?"

"Of course not." Grace grabbed the pile of charts off the seat and set them on top of the stack on her desk. "Have a seat."

This time she made her tone more approachable. After all, part of her job as director of the free clinic was to keep the physician volunteers happy. It wasn't always easy to find doctors willing to lengthen their already-overextended workday by several hours. Specialists were especially hard to find. Most tried it a couple of times and never came back. But Dr. Nick had been volunteering once a month at the specialty clinic for almost a year.

Though Grace had been the clinic director for the entire time, she couldn't say she really knew him.

Unlike Larry Fowler and some of the other doctors who'd hang around after clinic hours to talk, Nick Tucci always arrived right before his shift began and left immediately after seeing the last patient.

Once, when he'd raced by her yet again without even a hello, she casually mentioned his aloofness to Larry. Of course, Larry stood up for his colleague, mumbling something about Nick hating to keep patients waiting. Grace didn't buy that phony excuse for a minute. She knew if she looked like Cindy Crawford, he'd have found time to stop and talk. But a skinny redheaded thirty-year-old didn't rate a second glance.

"Busy evening," he said conversationally, his broad hands folded loosely in his lap.

Grace nodded. Every appointment slot had been filled this evening and most had been double-booked to cover the no-shows. Unfortunately every patient had shown up, which meant the staff were all getting out a lot later than usual.

Though Nick had never complained about working late before, she'd overheard him tell one of the nurses he'd been in surgery all morning. Her blood ran cold.

What if he wants to quit? What if that was why he'd stopped to talk?

"I'm sorry about the patient volume, but there's so much need in this neighborhood." Grace leaned forward, fear making the words tumble out one after the other. "You're doing a great job. And we appreciate it. I don't ever want you to think we take you for granted.''

He sat back in his chair and stared at her for a long moment. Grace realized for the first time that his eyes weren't hazel as she'd thought, but a mesmerizing blue-green color with flecks of gold. Feeling the need for some air, Grace took a deep breath and inhaled the spicy scent of his cologne.

''…giving back.''

Grace widened her eyes and realized that while she'd been staring at him, he'd been talking. Heat rose up her neck and she mentally kicked herself. No wonder handsome guys were arrogant, with women like her hanging on their every word. Or in her case, too busy gawking to hear anything at all. It was almost laughable. She, who'd always insisted she didn't like handsome men, was acting like a hormone-charged sixteen-year-old. Her lips twitched.

''You find that amusing?''

''Yes,'' she said. ''I mean no.''

Grace groaned to herself. Could she come across as any more of a blithering idiot than she did at this very moment? It hardly seemed possible. She brushed a piece of hair back from her face and tried to regain her composure.

Grace forced the disturbing images from her thoughts.

''I hear you're looking for a boyfriend.''

She tilted her head, sure she'd misunderstood. ''What did you say?''

"Larry told me you need a date for Thanksgiving weekend," he said. "Is that true?"

By now Grace's head was spinning. The doctor's ability to change the subject had her totally perplexed. "That's right. What about it?"

"Have you found anyone yet?"

She shook her head. Last month when she'd decided to bite the bullet and go home for the holiday, she'd started looking for a date. At the time she didn't think she'd have any trouble finding someone. After all, she had a lot of guy friends and she didn't care who came with her.

Unfortunately, one by one, the men she'd had in mind turned her down. Oh, they'd all had good reasons, but the fact was she was stuck. She'd told her family she'd be bringing her new boyfriend. How could she say she was coming alone? Again.

Turning thirty was bad enough. But to show up all by herself when her little sister, Holly, would be there with her husband and new baby? No way.

Grace knew she was being silly and immature. She had so many things to be grateful for: good health, good friends and a rewarding job. Not having a boyfriend was such a minor thing in the grand scheme of life. So many people had so much less. She saw it at her job every day.

But still, all she'd ever wanted was to be a wife and mother. And she couldn't understand how her sister had ended up with her dream life. It was as if God had gotten the two sisters' prayers mixed up. Holly had been determined to have a career. But she'd fallen in love while she was still in college and married shortly after graduation. Anna had been born on Holly's fifth wedding anniversary.

Grace, meanwhile, had a career, but no husband or family. And last month she'd hit the big three-oh with no Mr. Right in sight.

"Grace?"

Once again the deep voice beckoned her back to the present.

"I apologize," she said, rapidly collecting her thoughts. "Where were we?"

"I asked if you'd found someone to go home with you for Thanksgiving," he said with an indulgent smile. "You said you hadn't."

Grace raised a brow.

"The point is, I've found someone to go with you," he said.

Grace tried to still her excitement. Thanksgiving was only two days away and she'd almost given up hope. Grace leaned forward, resting her forearms on the table. "Who is he?"

"Me." Nick sat back and smiled. "I'll go with you."

Grace's cheeks burned like she'd just been slapped. Hard. She tried to stem her embarrassment, but when she spoke, humiliation made her voice harsh and tight. "What kind of game are you playing? Did Larry put you up to this?"

Nick met her gaze with a puzzled look. "I'm not playing any game."

"*You* want to go with *me?*" Grace shook her head. "I don't get it."

"It's true," Nick said lightly. "I'm at loose ends this weekend, and getting away from it all sounds like just what the doctor ordered."

Grace stared, wondering what kind of bet he had with Larry. She could just imagine the two laughing their heads off in the back room, thinking she'd be stupid enough to snap up the bogus offer.

She pressed her lips together to still the trembling. She'd never had someone play such a cruel trick on her before.

Nick's smile faded. He pushed back the chair and slowly rose to his feet, staring at her for a long moment. "If you don't want me to go with you, just say so."

He met her gaze head-on and his tone was so sincere Grace wondered if she'd been mistaken. After all, though he'd been aloof, she'd never known him to be mean. She took a chance and offered him a tiny smile. "It's not that. It's just it's hard for me to understand why you would give up your Thanksgiving to come to Iowa with me."

"My sister is playing matchmaker again," he said, resuming his seat. "I'm not in the mood. It's been a hectic couple of months and I just want to relax. Eat some turkey, have some pie…" He stopped suddenly and frowned. "Your parents aren't vegetarian, are they?"

Grace had to laugh. Vegetarian? Her father wouldn't allow tofu in the house, and the only kind of beans he liked were baked with lots of bacon fat. "They're Iowa farmers. Real meat-and-potatoes kind of people."

"Meat and potatoes are good." Nick nodded approvingly. "What about pie?"

"Pumpkin, mince, pecan and cherry." Grace counted them off on her fingers. "With real whipped cream, of course."

"I love whipped cream," Nick said in a deliciously deep voice.

"I do, too." Grace returned his smile. And as she was pulled into the azure depths of his eyes, Grace realized she was about to do something incredibly stupid.

She was going to accept Nick Tucci's offer.

Chapter Two

The farmyard was filled with cars but Nick was able to find a spot for his Land Rover just east of the barn. Grace waited for Nick to open her car door. It hadn't taken her long to realize that the handsome Dr. Tucci was a rarity in today's modern world, a true gentleman. He'd insisted on carrying her overnight bag to the car and on opening the door. Though Grace could have easily handled either task, she had to admit she liked the pampering.

As they walked toward the house Grace slanted him a sideways glance. How a guy could look so good in a sweatshirt and blue jeans boggled her mind. The jeans were nothing special but the way they hugged his muscular legs did crazy things to Grace's pulse.

Of course she blamed her reaction on the fact that she'd rarely seen him in anything other than dress pants and a white lab coat. When he'd asked her what he should wear, she'd hesitated for a second before telling him honestly that holidays in the Comstock family were extremely casual and that most of the men would probably be wearing jeans and sweatshirts.

To his credit, he didn't act surprised but merely smiled and said something about it sounding good. She knew he was just being polite. His family was quite prominent in the St. Louis social scene and Grace had no doubt that Thanksgiving dinner in the Tucci household would include china, crystal and candlelight. Why, she wouldn't be surprised if they wore ties to the table.

Dear God, why did I ever think this would work?

"Looks like your dad farms quite a few acres." Nick's pleasant voice brought her back to the present.

"How'd you guess?" Grace hated talking farming but her stomach was a mass of nerves and she hoped some light conversation might have a settling effect.

Nick gestured with his head toward several large storage silos. "Those were my first clue."

His smile was so warm and friendly that Grace couldn't help but return it. And for a fleeting moment she forgot to worry about how she was going to make it through the weekend. Unfortunately, the minute she set foot on the front porch and heard the buzz of conversation from inside the house, her neck tightened into a thousand knots. "This was a mistake."

"Just relax." He treated her to a flash of dimples.

"These are your family members. If anyone should be nervous, it should be me."

Shame filled her. He was doing her a favor and all she'd been able to think about was herself. She hadn't for a moment considered that Nick might have some qualms about the weekend.

"Are you?" she asked. "Nervous, I mean?"

Nick shrugged. "Not really. I've played the boy-friend role enough in real life to have it down pat. I can do the devoted act in my sleep."

Though Grace smiled, his words were clearly a warning, one she'd better heed. It would be so easy to get caught up in this charade and forget it was just a game. She had to remember that men like Nick Tucci only fell for the girl-next-door plain-Jane type in the movies, not in real life.

She reached for the screen door, but Nick beat her to it. "Allow me."

A moment later, Grace stood in the doorway to the home that had been in her family since the early 1900s and inhaled the atmosphere. The grandfather clock her father had built stood in one corner. The lace doilies her mother had tatted one summer graced the antique side table. Everything was so familiar. An overwhelming urge to call it all off nipped at her tightly held control.

How many times had she imagined bringing home a handsome man to meet her parents? How many times had she prayed that God would send her a man she could love and respect? How many times had she told herself to be patient and remember that things happen in God's time?

So what was she doing stooping to a childish game of Let's Pretend? Though Nick had already brought their bags inside and set them down in a corner of the foyer, Grace was seized with a sudden urge to flee.

As if Nick could read her mind, he reached up and rested his hand gently on her neck, rubbing it with slow circular motions. The mere touch of his fingers forced all rational thoughts from her head.

"Relax." His voice was as low and soothing as his fingers. "We can pull this off."

We.

Grace released the breath she hadn't realized she'd been holding and reminded herself she wasn't in this alone. For whatever reason, Nick had consented to be a part of this charade.

Propelled by emotions she couldn't begin to identify, Grace turned toward the man and lifted her face to his.

The appreciation in his eyes took her by surprise and she took a stumbling step backward. She would have fallen if he hadn't grasped her arm, offering her a steadying hand.

"Gracie."

Grace's heart stilled.

Nosy Nellie had spotted them.

Grace forced a smile to her face and gave a casual wave even as her heart sank. She'd known she'd have to face her aunt sometime this weekend, but she hadn't planned to be torpedoed the minute she and Nick walked through the door of the family farmhouse.

Grace knew it was ridiculous, the way her stomach twisted in knots over a middle-aged woman in a purple jogging suit.

But this wasn't just any woman. Her mother's sister had been meddling in Grace's life since she'd had the unfortunate luck to be born with her aunt's coppery red hair. According to her mother, Nellie had wept with joy, declaring God had blessed her with a child after all.

Grace thought her mother should have put a stop to such nonsense from the beginning. But the two sisters were close and her mother turned a blind eye to Nellie's domineering ways. To be honest, Grace had enjoyed having two "mothers" when she was very young. But by the time she'd reached her teens, her aunt had become an interfering thorn in her side.

Grace had quickly learned it did no good to complain. Her parents had quoted Leviticus 19:32 so much, the verse was permanently imprinted in her brain.

She should have warned Nick about Nellie. But what could she say? *My aunt looks sweet but she can be a pit bull when she's riled?* No, it was best he find out for himself. Maybe Nellie would be on her good behavior this weekend. And then again, maybe pigs would fly.

Grace grabbed his arm and tried to divert Nick toward the kitchen, but she was too late. He'd caught sight of Nellie weaving unsteadily as she made her way toward them and had stepped forward to help.

Nellie's shakiness was highly suspicious. Though hampered by a recent knee surgery, when Grace had first walked through the door, she'd seen Nellie maneuvering through the crowded living room with a quickness and dexterity that Michael Jordan would have envied. But all of a sudden, she could barely stand?

Nick reached out and her aunt clung to his arm, like he was a life preserver and she was about to go under for the last time.

"Nick, she's fine," Grace said. "Really."

But Nick ignored her and kept hold of Nellie's arm. "Are you okay, ma'am?"

Nellie's bony legs trembled beneath the silky fabric and Grace wondered for a second if she'd been too quick to assume her aunt had been faking. But then she remembered the time Nellie had faked an asthma attack to keep Grace from going to an after-hours high school party. By the time Grace had figured out the scam, she'd already called 9-1-1 and had the fire trucks at the house.

"Gracie." Nellie opened her arms. "I've missed you."

"It's been a long time," Grace murmured, giving her aunt a dutiful hug.

Nellie clung to her for a moment before she stepped back and held Grace at arm's length, her eyes large and pale behind the thick tortoiseshell trifocals. "I was worried you wouldn't come."

"I wouldn't have missed it for the world." The lie slid easily from Grace's lips. "This is my first chance to see Holly and the baby."

"I'm glad to hear you're taking this all this so well," Nellie said. "I worried this year might be difficult for you, being single and all. That's why I was glad to hear you were bringing a young man. It can be hard for the older sister when the younger one has a husband and a family and she has no special—"

"Aunt Nellie, really, it's no problem." Her aunt's words hit too close to home and Grace spoke more sharply than she'd intended. "I don't need a man to feel okay about myself."

Her aunt's smile faded and Grace cursed her impulsivity. Regardless of how she felt about her aunt's meddling, there was no call to be unkind.

"You may not need us—" Nick looped his arm companionably around Grace's shoulders "—but you have to admit, we're kind of nice to have around."

Grace cast Nick an appreciative smile. His off-the-wall comment had clearly eased the tension.

"You must be Gracie's new boyfriend." Nellie cocked her head and studied Nick, a smile teasing the corners of her lips.

Grace tensed, ready for the game of Twenty Questions to begin.

"Nick Tucci." Nick extended his hand. "And you are—?"

Grace groaned. She must be more nervous than she'd thought to have forgotten her manners. "Nick, this is—"

"Eleanora Best," Nellie said, without waiting for Grace to finish. "Gracie's aunt."

"Pleased to meet you, Mrs. Best," Nick said, his voice filled with such sincerity, Grace could only stare. She could see why all the women at the hospital were half in love with him. The man had charm down to a science.

"It's *Miss* Best," Nellie said, her smile widening. "But you can call me Nellie."

"Nellie." Nick rolled the word around on his tongue. He shook his head. "It just doesn't fit. May I call you Eleanora?"

Nellie's eyes widened in surprise and Grace waited for her aunt to snap back some tart reply. Instead a pink duskiness touched Nellie's cheeks. "If you'd like."

Grace stared at her aunt. "I don't think I've ever heard anyone call you Eleanora."

"No one has in years," Nellie said, a faraway look in her eyes. "Not since I was about your age."

"Well, it's time they started," Nick said gallantly. "It's a beautiful name and it suits you."

A noise that sounded suspiciously like a giggle escaped her aunt's lips. "Mr. Tucci, I can see my niece is going to have trouble keeping you in line."

"Eleanora," Nick said in a teasing tone, "I insist you call me Nick."

"Nick." Her aunt rolled the name around on her tongue, just like Nick had done only moments before. "Nicholas is much more of gentleman's name. May I call you Nicholas?"

Grace stared. Either she was hallucinating or her sixty-year-old aunt was flirting.

Nick laughed. "I never could refuse a beautiful lady."

"Nicholas," her aunt said in mock warning even as her laughter mingled with his. When Nellie's gaze shifted to her niece, approval filled her eyes. "I like him, Gracie. This one's a keeper."

Grace just smiled and nodded. If her aunt wanted to see Nick Tucci as a knight in shining armor, so be it. But Grace lived in the real world and Nick was the type of man Grace had spent most of her dating life avoiding; handsome men who asked women out only to stand them up if something better came along, or who automatically expected sex as payment for dinner and a movie.

Nick leaned over and brushed her cheek with his lips. "What do ya say, Gracie? Am I a keeper?"

His touch sent a shiver of excitement racing through her body, but Grace kept a tight grip on her emotions, refusing to get sucked into whatever game he was playing.

Grace turned toward him and trailed a finger down his cheek, hiding a smile at the surge of masculine interest in his eyes. "Nich-o-las Tucci, I'd be a fool to answer that question. You are already way too arrogant for your own good."

He laughed. "Arrogant or not, you know you still love me."

"Does the term 'in your dreams' mean anything to you?" Grace shot back.

"Gracie." Nellie's hand rose to her throat, her voice filled with shock.

"Don't worry, Eleanora." Nick pulled Grace close

and chuckled. "I like a woman who plays hard to get."

The spicy scent of his cologne enveloped her and her knees grew weak.

"Just so she doesn't play too hard to get that you lose interest," Nellie said, shooting her niece a warning glance.

"Believe me, Aunt Nellie, I know what I'm doing." But despite her self-confident demeanor, Grace was anything but confident. She knew as well as she knew her own name that Nick was way out of her league.

He was too good-looking for his own good. If you believed the gossip in the hospitals, he'd dated half the women in St. Louis and bedded most of them. She, on the other hand, had dated only two men in the last five years. Both had been brief and unremarkable relationships. Neither of them had ever made her heart beat faster, the way Nick had just done.

She shifted her gaze to the handsome dark-haired stranger at her side. Maybe it would have been best to come alone, to spend the weekend enduring endless questions and comments from well-meaning relatives about her unmarried state.

Because she had the sinking feeling that in bringing Nick with her, she may have just have exchanged one problem for another.

Chapter Three

The steady rhythmic tick of the bedside clock filled Grace's childhood bedroom. Though the aging mattress was comfortable, and the feather pillow fluffy, Grace found it difficult to sleep.

Tomorrow afternoon, just after church, she and Nick would head back to St. Louis. Never had four days flown by so quickly. It was hard to believe the weekend she'd dreaded for so long was over.

Having a "boyfriend" along had definitely put a halt to all those "When are you going to find someone?" questions. Unfortunately now she had a whole new set of questions to face.

In fact, Grace had barely gotten through the introductions when her sister had pulled her aside and asked with barely concealed excitement, "Where did you find him? He's gorgeous."

Her mother had been more subtle. Though her eyes had been filled with curiosity, she'd patiently waited until she and Grace were alone in the kitchen. Then, casting a furtive look at the door, she'd lowered her voice and asked in an offhand tone, that Grace guessed was anything but offhand, if she and Nick were serious.

It had been all Grace could do to keep a straight face. She couldn't believe her mother was so gullible. She should know better. Handsome men weren't attracted to average women.

But Grace had simply shrugged and said they had a good time together and who knew what might happen? After all, Nick was putting on the performance of a lifetime. She couldn't blame her mother for wondering if wedding bells weren't far off.

She'd tried to tell Nick to tone it down a few degrees and that all he needed to pretend to be was her "good" friend, but he said it was more fun to pretend to be more.

More.

The word sent a tingle of excitement up Grace's spine. All weekend she'd tried hard to not be affected by Nick's casual displays of affection. But when he'd catch her eye and smile, or when he'd grab her hand and bring it to his lips, her heart had pounded so hard, she could barely breathe. She could scarcely imagine what would happen if he actually kissed her, *really* kissed her....

A light knock sounded at the door and Grace jerked upright in bed.

"Are you awake?" Nick's deep voice carried easily though the door.

Grace hurriedly pushed back the quilted comforter. Her parents and aunt were just down the hall, and if they weren't already awake, they would be soon. What was Nick doing up? And, more importantly, what was he doing at her bedroom door?

"Just a minute." Unlike Nick, Grace spoke in hushed tones, loud enough for him to hear, but hopefully not loud enough to carry through the door and down the hall.

She swung her legs to the side of the bed and pushed her feet into a pair of pink furry slippers with bunny ears. Grabbing her chenille robe from the foot of the bed, she hurried across the shiny wood floor. By the time she reached the door, the belt of the robe was cinched tight and her curiosity was fully aroused.

"Grace?"

"Hold on." Wishing she had time for a quick look in the mirror, Grace contented herself with just running her fingers through her hair. Taking a deep breath, she pulled the door open.

Nick stood in the dimly lit hall, barefoot, dressed in a pair of plaid flannel pajama pants and a loose-fitting T-shirt.

Grace tilted her head. "What's up?"

The greeting came out casual and offhand, as if having a half-dressed man knocking on her bedroom door in the middle of the night was nothing out of the ordinary.

Nick gave her a lazy smile and the dimple in his cheek flashed. His dark hair was mussed like he'd just gotten up and hadn't taken the time to comb it. He looked, she thought, simply incredible. "Can I come in?"

A shiver traveled up Grace's spine. At that moment she wanted nothing more than to throw caution to the wind and invite him in. But she couldn't. It wouldn't be a smart move. And Grace was a smart woman. "Ummm, no."

Surprise flickered in his eyes and she could tell *no* was a word he didn't usually hear from females. "We need to talk."

Grace crossed her arms across her chest and shot him an impish smile. "Somehow I don't think talking is what you have in mind."

To her surprise, Nick burst into laughter.

Loud laughter.

Horrified, all Grace could think of was her aunt just two doors down. She grabbed Nick's arm and pulled him into the room, shutting the door behind him.

"You have to keep it down," she said in a tense whisper. "You'll wake the whole house."

Nick smiled, apparently not at all worried by the possibility. "We're both adults. Anyway, do you really think your parents would be shocked to find a man in your bedroom?"

Grace thought quickly. She didn't want to come across as a total prude. "They don't believe in sex before marriage. This is their house."

"I realize this is their house," Nick said. "But

don't try to tell me they believe you've never slept with a man.''

"Of course they believe that." Grace tried to still her rapidly beating pulse, but his closeness made that impossible.

Nick started to chuckle, then stopped. He stared at Grace for a long moment. "Is it true?"

She rolled her eyes and forced a laugh. "What do you think?"

It wasn't exactly lying. More like hedging. She hated to not tell the truth, but if she did, he'd think she was weird. Or frigid.

Nick smiled.

Her heart flip-flopped in her chest.

Suddenly unsure of the wisdom of her lie, Grace nervously brushed a strand of hair back from her face. "I'm still waiting to hear why you're here."

"I couldn't sleep." His gaze remained fixed on hers. "I thought you might like to take a walk."

Grace glanced at the bedside clock. "It's three-thirty in the morning."

"It's a beautiful night," Nick said, flashing her an enticing smile. "Clear—"

"Cold."

"Minimal snow," Nick continued without missing a beat. "Just grab—" his gaze lowered to her bunny slippers "—some shoes."

"Maybe Flopsy and Mopsy want to go for a walk." Grace wiggled her feet back and forth, causing the long pink ears at the top of her slippers to wiggle.

Nick chuckled.

Grace smiled and leaned over, trying to fix Mopsy's bent ear. It took a few seconds—one of the inside wires had started to protrude—but when she straightened she found Nick's gaze had not wavered. When she followed the direction of his gaze she realized it wasn't the slippers that had captured his attention, but something else. When she'd leaned over, her robe had fallen open, revealing her satin nightgown.

Her cheeks burning, Grace casually reached up and adjusted the robe.

"I never pegged you for the satin type," Nick said as if they were discussing her taste in food rather than her taste in lingerie.

Grace lifted a brow but remained silent, vaguely irritated by the comment, but not sure why.

Her gaze dropped to his flannel pajama pants. They were a well-known brand and very stylish. In fact she'd bought a similar pair for her brother-in-law last month for his birthday.

"I guess we're even then," she said.

"Even?" His gaze grew puzzled.

"I never pegged you as a flannel kind of guy."

"I'm not." Nick grinned. Surprisingly he didn't seem the least bit upset by her observation. "These were my one concession to the weekend."

"You bought new pajamas just for the weekend?" Grace asked. "Why would you do that?"

Even as she asked the question, Grace realized the answer. She lifted her gaze and could see the confirmation in Nick's twinkling smile and wicked grin. So he normally slept…without pajamas.

Before she could process the information, he took a step closer and his hand briefly cupped her face.

Grace knew Nick was going to kiss her. She could see it in his eyes. And though she could have just taken a step back, Grace didn't move an inch.

Because all weekend long she'd wanted this to happen. When she'd gone to bed earlier she'd thought the opportunity had passed. Tomorrow they'd be back in St. Louis. He'd go his way. She'd go hers.

Now it appeared she was being given another chance. An unexpected opportunity to assuage her curiosity about kissing Nick Tucci.

Nick now stood so close she couldn't help but breathe in his delicious scent. He wasn't wearing cologne, but the mixture of the shampoo and soap he used was better than any bottled aroma.

Kissing him in her bedroom might not be the smartest thing to do, but Grace didn't worry about things getting out of hand. After all, she was curious, nothing more.

But when his hand gently brushed her hair from her face, her breath caught in her throat. And when his lips gently brushed hers then pulled back, she quivered with disappointment. That wasn't the type of kiss she expected. She'd wanted…

Suddenly his lips returned, moving gently against hers as if he expected her to shut him down at any minute. Grace found the slight hesitation strangely endearing.

She looped her arms around his neck and his arms tightened about her. There was now no space between them, no way they could get any closer.

Grace absorbed the feel of him, the way his muscles flexed beneath her palms, the slight scratch of whisker stubble against her cheek.

Her fingers wove their way through the soft texture of his hair as his mouth closed over hers.

This time his lips lingered, caressing her mouth, drawing her into a whirling spiral of emotions and sensations she'd never felt before. She returned his kisses breathlessly, barely conscious of the fact that while they were kissing, his hands were gently caressing her shoulders and stroking her back.

Grace shivered, the response at odds with the heat searing her skin. Though she knew she should end this madness now, she couldn't bring herself to do it. Not yet.

Her heart raced and she struggled to keep her breathing steady as his lips closed over hers again.

Then he deepened the kiss and her world exploded. It was like she was drowning and soaring at the same time. She moaned, a low sound that astonished her with its intensity. Dazed and breathing hard, Grace pulled away.

''Grace?'' Nick's eyes were so dark, they almost looked black.

Grace shifted her gaze and crossed her arms, a chill traveling through her body. What had she been thinking? It was bad enough she'd let Nick into her room knowing his reputation. But to kiss him like that...

She drew a ragged breath. "I think you'd better..."

"Grace." A sharp rap sounded at the door. "Is everything okay?"

Aunt Nellie.

Grace's heart stopped even as her mind raced. She couldn't let Nellie find Nick in her bedroom. Her aunt was old school. She'd never understand it was all completely innocent.

"Everything's fine, Aunt Nellie." Grace moved to the door and forced a reassuring tone.

"But I heard noises," Nellie said. "I was worried."

Grace slanted a glance back at Nick. He looked like every woman's fantasy standing next to her bedpost, his arms crossed against his chest. If her aunt was worried now, what would she be if found Nick in her niece's bedroom?

"There's nothing to worry about," Grace said, leaning her head against the door, the words flowing easily despite the tightness in her throat. "I was having difficulty sleeping, so I got up. I'm sorry if my moving about woke you. I'll try to be more quiet."

There was silence on the other side of the door and for a second, Grace thought she was home free. Her aunt would go back to her own room and Nick would go back to his. She would go back to her own bed and try to forget how close she'd come to disaster.

"May I come in for a second?" Nellie asked.

Though her aunt had phrased the request as a question, the tone was more along the lines of "Open the door—I'm coming in."

Grace stifled a groan and glanced around the room. Though hiding a man in the closet seemed a bit melodramatic, Grace didn't have a choice.

The situation reminded Grace of a soap opera. And some might even find it amusing. But Grace didn't see anything even remotely funny about her current predicament.

"Let me just grab my robe," Grace said, stalling for time.

She padded silently across the room to the louvered closet door and gestured to Nick.

He stared, but didn't move.

"Get inside," she mouthed, pointing first at him and then at the closet.

For a moment, Grace thought he wasn't going to comply. But the look in her eye must have convinced him of the seriousness of the situation because he entered the closet and let her shut the door.

Grace cinched the robe tight about her and squared her shoulders. Then, feeling like Daniel about to face the lions, she opened the bedroom door.

Nick sat on the cold hardwood floor and knew he had to be dreaming. What other reason would there be for a respected physician and surgeon to be hiding in a closet?

It wasn't as if he was fooling around with a married woman, something he'd never consider doing. Marriage vows were sacred.

He glanced around the half-empty closet. Personally he thought Grace was being ridiculous. But he'd seen the determined look on her face and he knew she'd never forgive him if he didn't go along.

Nick had to smile. He was learning that with Grace, you never knew quite what to expect. He still couldn't believe he'd worked with her for almost a year and had never really known her. He'd been intrigued from the start. And with that copper-colored hair and big green eyes, she'd been hard to miss. But she'd always been all business.

When they'd said good night earlier this evening and gone to their separate bedrooms, he'd had the feeling that whatever had existed between them this weekend was over. Tomorrow he'd go back to his life and she'd go back to hers. It would be as if this time together had never happened.

And that made him sad. This weekend had been a revelation. The more he'd gotten to know Grace, the more he'd realized how much they had in common.

Unfortunately, Grace didn't seem to feel the same way. Nick hated to say it, but Larry had been right. Grace didn't like him. Not very much anyway.

It was puzzling. To his knowledge, he'd never done anything to offend her. And this weekend, he'd played the part of adoring boyfriend with such passion he'd thought she'd have been pleased.

But though she smiled up at him and let him hold her hand whenever he'd wanted, emotionally she'd kept her distance. And that drove him crazy.

He'd come to her room, for what he wasn't quite sure. Maybe to clear the air. Maybe to find some common ground. Maybe to sneak a few kisses. But when he'd seen the satin nightgown against all that creamy freckle-spattered skin, he'd wanted to do more than just kiss her. It had been a long time since he'd felt such an overwhelming need.

Oh, he'd dated lots of women but he could count on one hand the ones he'd been intimate with. He was very particular about who he got involved with. He wanted a relationship, not a quick fling.

"People thought you'd made up a boyfriend." Though Nellie spoke in low tones, her voice carried clearly through the slats in the closet door.

"Did they?" Grace's laugh sounded forced. "I can't imagine why."

"It can be quite a blow when the youngest sister marries first," Nellie said. "And then when she has a child—"

"It didn't bother me," Grace said quickly, too quickly.

"Not at all?" Nellie's tone was clearly skeptical.

"Not at all," Grace said firmly.

Nick smiled. He didn't know who was more stubborn—Grace or her aunt Nellie.

"Of course, you've got Nick," Nellie said in a conversational tone.

"That's right," Grace said after what seemed like a long silence. "I've got Nick."

Nick released the breath he didn't realize he'd been holding. It was a forced admission and one that meant nothing.

But it was a start. Something to build on. Because Nick was certain what he'd told Larry was the truth. Grace didn't like him because she didn't really know him.

That's why he had to figure out a way to keep seeing her when they returned to St. Louis.

Time was what he needed.

Unfortunately, right now it was the one thing he didn't have.

Chapter Four

Nellie's youngest niece popped her head into the kitchen where Nellie sat sipping a cup of Earl Grey. "Have you seen my mother?"

Nellie glanced up from the Milestones section of the *Des Moines Register*.

"She ran next door for a few minutes." When Holly lingered in the doorway, Nellie laid the paper down and turned her attention from the wedding and anniversary announcements to her niece. "Is there anything I can help you with?"

"Not really." Holly shook her head. "Anna has some red bumps on her bottom and I wanted Mom to see them before I got her dressed."

Nellie almost said that it sounded like diaper rash and that she'd be glad to take a look. But at the last minute, she bit back the words. Holly obviously wanted to tap into her mother's experience—a woman who'd raised two children—rather than settle for the opinion of a childless aunt. The fact that Nellie had helped raise both Holly and her sister wouldn't make a difference; she wasn't a *mother.*

"I'll tell Margaret to come to your room the minute she gets back." Nellie shot her clearly worried niece a reassuring smile. "I'm sure Anna will be fine until then."

The concern that had gripped Holly's pretty face eased. Though Holly had just turned twenty-six, Nellie couldn't help but think Holly looked much too young to have a husband and baby.

"That'd be great," Holly said. "I need to finish getting ready for church anyway. You can't believe how much work it is to get a baby bathed and dressed."

Nellie just smiled. Any infant was a lot of work, but Holly and Tim had been blessed. Anna was a placid, good-natured baby who only cried when she needed to be changed or fed. Not all babies were so easy.

Nellie's thoughts drifted back to her first vision of Grace, screaming and waving her little hands in the hospital nursery. Her face had been almost as red as her hair. Up to that point Nellie had been the only redhead in the family. She'd fallen in love with her new niece instantly.

In fact, Nellie had celebrated her thirtieth birthday walking the floor with the colicky infant. Margaret had been in bed with the flu and Hal, Margaret's husband, had been out of town.

Even though she didn't get much sleep that night,

Nellie had loved every minute of it. In the still, dark house—for that brief moment in time—Nellie had pretended God had answered her prayers and given her a child of her own.

It was a brief respite from the fear that had dogged her thoughts every time she'd thought of her birthday. The realization that she was starting her fourth decade on earth had forced Nellie to take stock of her situation all those years ago.

At thirty she had been definitely past her prime. She had known the odds were high that a Prince Charming would never come to her door, that there would not be any babies for her to love, that she would spend the rest of her life alone.

It was different now; women married later and had children well into their thirties and forties.

But back then the realization that life had passed her by had been hard to bear. She only had to look at her sister's life to see what could have been.

Because not only did God bless her sister with one baby, several years later He blessed her with another little girl. Holly was born shortly after Grace's fourth birthday, with a head full of curly blond hair and a sweet, sunny disposition. Everyone adored Holly, and Nellie was no exception. But it was the more serious, sensitive older child who held Nellie's heart in the palm of her hand.

Maybe it was because Nellie understood Grace's awkward shyness. After all, she'd been burdened with the same malady. Maybe it was because Nellie had also been a studious "bookworm" as a child. Or maybe it was because she could identify with Grace's pain. No one knew better than Nellie how hard it could be to grow up in the shadow of a beautiful and popular younger sister.

At Holly's wedding five years ago, Nellie's tears of joy were mixed with sadness. Grace was the oldest. She should have married first.

Just like I should have married before Margaret.

In the last few years Nellie had started to worry Grace might be headed down the same lonely path she'd traveled. But when Grace had shown up this weekend with an eligible bachelor on her arm, Nellie had experienced a resurgence of hope.

She'd tried not to get too excited because Grace had introduced him only as her "friend" and not as her "fiancé." But even though he hadn't yet put a ring on her finger, Nellie could see that Nicholas was a good, decent man who truly cared for her niece. Though she knew it might be a bit premature, Nellie couldn't help mentally jotting down a few names for the wedding guest list.

As far as Nellie was concerned, wedding bells couldn't be far off. Her vision might not be twenty-twenty anymore but she could see the way Nicholas's eyes glowed when he looked at Grace.

He admired her.

He adored her.

He desired her.

Nellie's lips tightened as a surge of motherly protectiveness raced through her. Desire was all well and good…if a couple were married. But Nicholas and

Grace weren't—not yet anyway—and his sneaking into Grace's room in the middle of the night had to stop. Nothing good came of intimacy before marriage.

Nellie suspected that bridge hadn't yet been crossed, but she wasn't sure how long her niece could hold out. The air fairly sizzled when the two of them were together. Though Grace had been taught right from wrong, Nicholas was a handsome, charming man and Nellie feared the temptation might prove too great.

If Grace were living in town, Nellie could act as a chaperone and keep things in check until vows were spoken. But with Grace living in St. Louis, Nellie was powerless to help.

Unless…

Nellie shifted in her chair. Hadn't her doctor suggested she consult a specialist about her knee problems? And hadn't Grace once told her the medical care in St. Louis was second to none?

Though Nellie normally liked to stay put in the cold weather, she was suddenly in the mood to travel. And at this point she couldn't think of a place she'd rather be than St. Louis.

The minister's message had centered around one of Grace's favorite Bible passages, but now, standing outside the white clapboard structure, Grace couldn't remember a single word of the sermon. And if she had to blame someone for her inattention, it would have to be Nick.

First, she'd gotten almost no rest last night. Though Nick had left shortly after Aunt Nellie, Grace had found it difficult to sleep. The unfamiliar sensations that he'd awakened had been difficult to quiet.

Then he'd come down the stairs this morning in a dark suit she swore was hand tailored. It had been the first time she'd seen him ''dressed up.'' Her breath had caught in her throat. Had there ever been a better-looking man? She realized to her horror that she'd been staring when he'd given her a wink and that cute little dimple in his left cheek had flashed.

It had been downhill from there. Since the community church was only a few blocks away and the weather was a balmy fifty, they'd decided to walk. Nick had insisted on taking her arm. And he'd insisted on teasing her the entire way to the church. Even though she didn't think she looked ''especially beautiful'' or ''delightfully sexy,'' his outrageous compliments had thrown her off balance.

By the time they'd gotten to the church, the service was ready to start and they'd had to squeeze into one of the far back pews. Nick's leg had been pressed so tightly against hers that they might have been fused together. Just the thought of being that close to Nick did funny things to her insides and made it difficult to give her full attention to the church's mission challenges in Haiti.

And now he stood in the shadow of the cross, with his hand proprietarily on her waist, conversing with people she'd known all her life, giving them the impression they were…a couple.

But that's why he's here. That's why you brought him with you.

But I didn't think it would be like this, Grace wanted to say. I didn't think it would be this hard.

Even to a cynic like her, Nick's excellent acting abilities made it all too believable.

"Where do you attend church, Mr. Tucci?" Pastor Steve's question brought Grace back to the present with a jerk.

Grace held her breath, wondering what he'd say. She and Nick had never discussed faith issues. After all, it wasn't as if they were really dating. And there had been more pressing issues related to the weekend that took priority when they'd been getting acquainted. But now Grace wished she'd at least touched on the topic. At this point she could only pray he wasn't an atheist, or if he was that he was smart enough not to mention the fact.

"King of Kings in St. Louis," Nick said. "I'm sure you haven't heard of it but—"

"Actually I know the church quite well," Pastor Steve interrupted. "One of my friends from seminary, John Richards, is head of the music ministry there."

"Pastor Richards has done a fabulous job with that program," Nick said with an easy smile. "My sister-in-law Sara is really into music and does a lot of work with John."

The two men continued talking. Grace could only stare. Nick had surprised her once again.

"I wondered if he was a Christian," Nellie said, nodding her approval, and Grace realized with a start that Nellie was standing right beside her. "I guess I have my answer."

"What does it matter?" Grace murmured to herself, knowing once this weekend was over, her encounters with "Dr. Nick" would be confined to the third Tuesday of every month when he did his specialty clinic.

"What does it matter?" Nellie's eyes widened and her voice rose. "If you and Nicholas are considering a future together, it means everything."

But we aren't, Grace wanted to cry out. Aunt Nellie needed to wake up and smell the coffee. Men like Nick Tucci could have any woman they wanted.

Suddenly Grace was tired of all the subterfuge. The weekend was over and she was ready for the lies to end. "It doesn't matter because I don't think Nick and I will be together much longer."

Though Grace had intended the whispered declaration to be matter-of-fact, the heavy sigh punctuating the words gave them a melancholy feel.

Nellie's brow furrowed. She reached over and patted Grace's arm in an awkward gesture of comfort. "If God intends for you to be with Nicholas, you'll be with him."

"That's a good thought," Grace said, her heart warmed by her aunt's support, however misguided. "But Nick's just not my type of guy."

Or more to the point, I'm not his type of woman.

"Has he been pushing you to be intimate?" Though Nellie spoke in a normal conversational tone, her gaze was sharp and assessing.

Grace's mouth dropped open. Then, regaining her composure she snapped her mouth shut and glanced around, hoping no one had heard the ridiculous question.

Unfortunately, like Grace's, her aunt's voice had always had a tendency to carry. And, coupled with the clear crisp autumn air and a lull in the surrounding conversations, the question rang out over the assembled throng.

Her parents turned as one and her father's eyes took on a protective gleam. Pastor Steve raised a brow. Holly gave a nervous giggle.

Grace could feel her face heat up and the only thing she could think of was Nick in her bedroom last night.

"No, no, of course not." Grace stumbled over the words, and even to her own ears she sounded unconvincing.

Thankfully, Nick refused to let her flounder. Though his eyes showed no trace of amusement, he chuckled. "What a ridiculous question. I respect Grace too much to ever push her to do something both of us know is wrong."

His tone was strong and firm, and if Grace didn't know better, even she would have believed him.

She couldn't help but be relieved when the tense

look on her father's face eased and her mother expelled the breath she must have been holding.

"I hope that's true," Nellie said, a silken thread of suspicion running through her words, leaving Grace to wonder if her aunt's "innocent" late-night visit might not have been quite so innocent after all.

Still, Grace shot her aunt a quelling glare. If Nellie had concerns, this was neither the time nor the place to air them.

Nick's gaze hardened. His arm rose to loop protectively about Grace's shoulders even as his gaze remained fixed on her aunt. "Eleanora."

The single word spoke volumes.

Nellie stared at Nick for a long moment. "If I judged you wrongly, I'm sorry."

It was a small concession, but Grace breathed a sigh of relief. Nick's arm relaxed against her shoulders and Grace realized that he'd been as unsure as she how Nellie would respond.

Giving her shoulder a reassuring squeeze, Nick turned his attention back to the minister as if their conversation had never been interrupted, leaving Grace alone with her aunt.

"What were you thinking of?" Grace said in a low tone between gritted teeth, even as she waved goodbye to a couple of high school friends across the parking lot.

Nellie's face reddened. "I didn't realize I'd spoken so loud."

But Grace refused to let her aunt off the hook so

easily. "Why even bring it up? And in front of the whole town, no less."

·Though Nellie had backed down from Nick, something in Grace's voice reignited the fire in her eyes. "Don't you talk to me in that tone, young lady. I am your aunt and deserving of your respect."

Grace could see her aunt was getting worked up and at any minute she expected Leviticus 19:32 to be quoted. But Grace didn't care. Nellie had embarrassed her. And she wasn't about to act like it didn't matter.

"Don't talk to me about respect," Grace said in a low tone, her gaze shifting to make sure no one was near enough to overhear. "You're the one who implied that I'm sleeping with Nick."

Even as Grace said the words, she knew they were a bit of an exaggeration. But they were close enough.

"Are you?" This time Nellie kept her voice to a mere whisper. "Have you and Nicholas—?"

"No," Grace said, cutting her aunt off. "No, we're not. And while we're talking about this, I don't know why you're even asking me such a question. Did you ask Holly that when she and Tim were dating?"

"I did not." Nellie's green eyes met Grace's. "I had no reason to suspect—"

"You have no reason—"

"—because I never saw Tim sneaking out of Holly's room in the middle of the night." Nellie completed the sentence as if she'd never been interrupted.

Grace stifled a groan even as she lifted her chin. "He wanted me to take a walk with him."

"He had on pajamas," Nellie said.

"They were flannel...." Grace started to explain, then gave up. "Believe what you want. It was all quite innocent."

"A man in a woman's bedroom is never completely innocent," Nellie said emphatically. "Can you honestly tell me you weren't tempted at all by—"

"He didn't pressure me," Grace said sharply, knowing she hadn't answered her aunt's question, but not caring. "That's what I said and that's what I meant. I refuse to discuss this another second."

"Okay." Nellie expelled a heavy sigh. "But remember that God said we should not put ourselves in the way of temptation. In the future, if Nicholas comes knocking on your door in the middle of the night, you shut the door in his face."

Just the idea of such an action should have been laughable, but Grace didn't feel like laughing. Because what Nellie didn't understand was once Grace returned to St. Louis, Nick wouldn't be at her door ever again.

"Okay, Aunt Nellie, I promise," Grace said. "If Nick ever comes by in the middle of the night again, I'll slam the door in his face."

"That's my girl." Nellie patted Grace's arm. "In the end he'll respect you for it."

"He'll do what?"

Grace turned in surprise. Apparently Nick must

have concluded his conversation with the minister and had shifted his focus back to Grace and Nellie. She wasn't sure how much he'd heard of their conversation but she definitely wasn't going to rehash it.

"I'm hoping you can refer me to a doctor in St. Louis," Nellie said. "To someone you know who is good with knees."

The request was so totally unexpected that not only Nick, but also Grace, was taken aback.

"I thought you just had surgery," Grace said.

"I did," Nellie answered. "But my knee isn't coming along as well as the doctor hoped and he thinks I need to see a specialist."

Grace's gaze shifted to Nick. "Do you know of someone?"

He nodded. "I have quite a few colleagues who specialize in knee problems."

"But they're all in St. Louis," Grace said. "There has to be someone closer you could see—"

"Of course there is," Nellie said with a dismissive wave. "But I don't know those people. Nicholas is in that field. I trust his recommendation."

"St. Louis is a long ways from here," Grace said, pointing out the obvious weakness in her aunt's argument. "How are you going to get there? Where will you stay?"

"Oh, my dear," Nellie said, casting Grace a pitying look as if the answer was so simple, she was a fool for not seeing it. "I'll ride back with you two. And I thought I'd stay with Nicholas. That is, if he'll have me after my faux pas this afternoon. I'm not sure at this point that I'd be able to handle those steps at your apartment.''

The horrified look on Grace's face brought a smile to Nick's lips. Though Grace had grown up around her aunt, he could tell Grace still hadn't figured the woman out.

But he had. This maneuver was clearly designed to keep him and Grace together. After all, if Nellie was living with him, Grace would see him every time she saw her aunt. The woman definitely had a devious mind when it came to matchmaking.

No wonder he'd liked her instantly.

''Aunt Nellie, I'm sure Nick doesn't want—''

Nick waved aside Grace's words. He shifted his gaze to the woman staring at him with a speculative gleam in her eyes.

He and Nellie were on the same wavelength. How could he not go along with her plan? Nick smiled. ''My house is your house.''

Chapter Five

The crystal glistened in the candlelight and the smell of fresh flowers filled the dining room of Nick Tucci's home.

Grace placed the linen napkin on her lap and took a sip of wine, wondering if the crystal and china were de rigueur in the Tucci household, or if Nick considered this a special occasion.

It was the first time she'd seen him in almost a week. Granted, things at the clinic had been in an uproar and she'd worked late almost every night since she'd returned from Iowa. But he could have made some effort to get in touch with her. Although from what Nellie told her, Nick had been putting in some long hours, too. So she shouldn't have felt slighted, but she did.

Still, she reminded herself, though he'd played the role of her boyfriend to perfection for four days and nights, it had only been a game. They'd had an agreement and he'd fulfilled it, end of story.

Then why did he kiss me? Why did he say he'd call?

Even as Grace asked the questions, she knew the answer. When he'd dropped her off after the long drive back, he'd been under a lot of pressure. Though her aunt had pretended to avert her gaze and had stayed in the car to give them some privacy, they both knew Nellie had been listening to their every word. The woman would have been disappointed if there had been no good-night kiss or promise to call.

Grace had expected a quick peck on the cheek. But Nick had pulled her into his arms and lowered his lips to hers. By the time he'd released her, Grace's mouth had been trembling and her head was spinning.

She'd called him several times since she'd gotten back, to thank him for being her "date." But she hadn't been able to reach him. Even the invitation for dinner tonight had come through his housekeeper.

Grace wondered if tonight's invitation was just Nick's good manners surfacing. She turned her attention away from the disturbing thought and smiled at her aunt. Nick had finagled an appointment with one of his colleagues for her aunt and Grace had been dying to hear the outcome. "Tell me about your appointment today. What did the doctor have to say?"

"Dr. Placek says he thinks I'll live," Nellie quipped, casting a smile in Nick's direction. "Actually he was very thorough and nice. He took more

X rays while I was there and asked me a bunch of questions.''

"He must have spent a long time with you," Grace said. "I tried to call you at three, but Nick's housekeeper said you weren't back yet."

"I was done with my visit around one." A tiny hint of pink touched her aunt's cheeks. "Then Paul took me out for a late lunch."

Grace widened her gaze, unable to hide her surprise. "Dr. Placek took you to lunch?"

Nellie laughed, a silvery tinkle of a laugh, and the color in her cheeks deepened. "Oh, my dear, no. Dr. Placek is scarcely older than you."

Grace looked at Nick, wondering if he was making sense of her aunt's remarks. A tiny smile tugged at the corners of his lips but he just took another sip of wine and shrugged.

"Okay, so I take it Paul is not Dr. Placek," Grace said. "But I still don't know who this Paul is or how you happen to know him."

"His name is Paul Morrow," her aunt said. "And he's an orthopedic doctor, too, but he specializes in hands, not knees."

"And how did you meet Dr. Morrow?" Grace kept her tone light and conversational, feeling like a mother trying to get details from a teenage daughter on a new boyfriend.

"Paul is a colleague of mine," Nick said, unexpectedly entering the conversation. "He stopped over the other night and I introduced them."

"When he heard I had an appointment in his office

building today, he graciously offered to take me to lunch," her aunt added.

Grace sat back in her chair. She couldn't remember her aunt ever dating, unless you counted Harold Peterman's occasional presence at her bridge foursome. "Sounds like you two really hit it off."

Nellie's lips curved in satisfaction. "If you're asking if we had a nice time, the answer is yes."

"He's not married, is he?" Grace hated to be blunt, but Nellie was a relative babe in the woods in the terms of dating, and she had no idea how devious men could be.

"Of course not." Nellie's hand rose to her throat and her eyes widened. "Paul is a gentleman."

Grace's skepticism must have still showed on her face because Nick chuckled.

"You can trust your aunt on this one. Paul would never have asked Eleanora to meet him for lunch if he was married," Nick said. "His wife died a couple of years ago and he's been alone ever since."

"I guess it all sounds on the up-and-up," Grace reluctantly conceded. "I don't know why I'm making such a big deal out of a lunch date, anyway. You'll probably never—"

The grandfather clock in the corner began to chime and Nellie glanced at her watch.

"I didn't realize it was so late." Nellie hurriedly pushed back her chair. "Paul will be picking me up at any moment and I'd like to freshen up before he gets here."

Grace stared dumbfounded while her aunt stood, an almost girlish smile on her lips.

"You have another date with him?"

Nellie's smile said it all. She gathered up her purse and left the room, a surprisingly lively spring to her step considering she was still nursing an injured knee.

"Two dates in one day." Grace shook her head and took another sip of wine.

Nick sat back in his chair, twirling the stem of the wineglass between his fingers. "Your aunt is a beautiful woman, not to mention bright and personable. Why is it so hard for you to believe a man would be interested in her?"

"That's not it at all." Grace chose her words carefully. "I'm just worried she'll get hurt."

"Why would she be hurt?" Nick asked.

"Because when you date, you get hurt," Grace said matter-of-factly. "It goes with the territory."

"I think that's a bit of an exaggeration," Nick said. "I've dated a lot of women and I've never been hurt."

"That's because you're a man," Grace said. "Women are the ones who get the short end of the stick."

Nick tilted his head and his brow furrowed. "So, have you gotten the short end of the stick?"

"A couple of times," Grace said. "But not lately. Now I know the score."

She'd had her first lesson in the ways of men her junior year in high school when Tommy Doyle had asked her to the prom, then promptly changed his mind. In college she'd dated John Tucker for three months without knowing he was engaged. Then there had been Steve...

Grace shoved the memory aside. She had nothing to complain about. She had friends who'd been hurt worse.

"I think you've let a few isolated instances color your feelings," Nick said.

"I think you're incredibly naive," Grace said, wondering why she'd ever let the conversation get on this track in the first place. The doorbell rang in a distant part of the house and she breathed a sigh of relief, grateful for an excuse to change the subject. "Do you think she'll ask Paul in?"

Nick shook his head. "They're going to the theater and they don't have much time."

Grace tried to hide her disappointment. She would have liked to have met her aunt's date. "I guess it's going to just be you and me for dinner."

"That's what I planned." Nick smiled his thanks as Mrs. Prescott placed the salads in front of them.

Grace realized for the first time that only she and Nick had silverware at their place settings.

"But when your housekeeper called, she said it would be the three of us."

"That was the original plan," Nick said smoothly. "Until your aunt met Paul."

"You didn't have to go to all this trouble just for me," Grace said.

"I wanted to see you," Nick said, pushing the

salad back and forth with his fork. "I've been so busy since I got back from Iowa, I haven't had a—"

"You don't need to make excuses." Grace waved aside his explanation. "Our arrangement was only for the weekend. I didn't really expect to see you again. Except at the clinic, of course."

For a moment Nick was silent and Grace had the odd feeling she might have offended him with her bluntness. But that was crazy. Because she was simply stating facts and letting him know she didn't expect anything at all from him.

"But what about…?" His voice trailed off and he nodded toward Nellie's empty chair.

"Good point," she said. "We should keep things up, at least while she's here. Unless you think we should tell her we broke up?"

"No," Nick said forcefully, then his tone softened. "Getting this orthopedic workup is hard enough on her. I wouldn't want to add to her stress."

Grace almost said that her aunt seemed quite laissez-faire about the appointments, but she stopped herself. Though it would probably be easiest on her own heart to break off all contact with Nick now, Grace couldn't do it. "I agree."

Her mood lightened at the thought of spending more time with him. He looked so good sitting there in his burgundy sweater and gray pants. If she didn't know it was impossible, she'd swear he was even more attractive than the last time she'd seen him, than the last time she'd been in his arms. She remembered the feel of his hair between her fingers, the taste of his lips, the—

"Are you finished with your salad, ma'am?"

Grace jerked back to the present with a start and lifted her gaze. Though the housekeeper's expression was inscrutable, the twinkle in her eyes told Grace the woman had a good idea where Grace's thoughts had been headed. "I am."

"But you only ate a few bites." Nick's dark brows furrowed in concern. "Are you feeling okay?"

"Yes, Doctor," Grace said with an impish smile. "I'm feeling quite well. I'm just not in the mood for lettuce."

His gaze met hers.

"What are you in the mood for?"

Suddenly she was back home in her bedroom with his arms wrapped around her. And she could see by the look in his eyes that he knew full well what she wanted.

It was crazy. It would be the height of stupidity to get involved with a man who could eventually break your heart.

But right now, with that heart beating double time and the air fairly humming with electricity, Grace couldn't walk away. In fact, she couldn't move at all.

"Mrs. Prescott," she heard Nick say through the roaring in her ears, "why don't you take the rest of the night off? We can serve ourselves."

"Very well, sir." Mrs. Prescott's hair might have been gray and her face wrinkled, but behind her thin wire rims, her gaze was keen and Grace guessed she missed very little.

Grace waited until the woman had left the room before she spoke. "She suspects something."

"Probably." Nick rose and circled the table coming to a stop beside Grace's chair. He held out his hand and feeling oddly breathless and extremely reckless, Grace pushed back her chair and stood. "She knows how much I like you."

Grace's breath caught in her throat. She paused, not sure she'd heard correctly. "What did you say?"

He wrapped his arms around her and pulled her close, heaving a contented sigh. "I said she knows how much I like you."

A warm rush of emotion flowed through her at the words. "Do you? Like me, I mean?"

He tipped her face to him and met her gaze before brushing her lips with his.

"For someone so smart—" he kissed her softly again "—you seem to have trouble getting the message. Let me see if I can make it clearer."

His arms tightened around her and she let him pull her close, resting her head against his chest, drawing comfort from the warmth of his arms.

"I've missed you." He pressed his face to her hair.

"I've missed you, too," she said. Her voice trembled with emotion.

Nick kissed her again, but this time his mouth lingered. Being in his arms again was heaven. His lips tasted like wine and Grace felt almost drunk with emotion.

With a start, Grace realized she was stroking the back of his neck, twining her fingers in his thick, soft hair. "Nick, I…"

He stopped her words by covering her mouth with his own. It was an exquisite kiss. Her lips parted before she had time to consider all of the ramifications of kissing Nick this way. And as Nick unhurriedly claimed her mouth, drinking her in, she stopped thinking.

She felt his hand move up her back, underneath her hair. His fingers sent both chills and warmth racing through her until she was nearly dizzy.

The quick rush of desire surprised her. How was it possible that she'd lived thirty years without ever feeling this, without knowing a kiss could be like this?

"Sir, I've…" Mrs. Prescott stopped short. She hurriedly placed two plates of food on the table then hastily backed out of the room. She was gone before either Nick or Grace could say a word.

Heat seared Grace's cheeks. She could only imagine what the housekeeper was thinking. Though the roast beef and potatoes smelled delicious, Grace knew she couldn't eat a bite. She pulled back from Nick's arms, her heart still racing. "I'd better go."

Grace started to move away, but Nick kept his arm around her waist. "Don't. She won't be back."

"It probably would have been better if she

stayed,'' Grace said. ''I think my aunt was right. You and I need a chaperone.''

Nick chuckled and took a step back. ''C'mon, it's just a kiss. That's what people do when they like each other.''

''It's not that simple,'' Grace said, wondering how she could possibly make him understand without giving her own feelings away. ''You kiss a lot of girls. I don't.''

His smile widened. ''I'm glad to hear that.''

It took her a minute to realize what she'd said. Grace groaned. ''You know what I mean.''

''You're wrong, you know.'' His eyes softened and he pushed her hair gently back from her face. ''I don't kiss a lot of girls.''

It was a nice thought and although she wished it was true, Grace wasn't stupid. ''Okay, so maybe they're women, not girls.''

Nick laughed and his dimple flashed. He tugged on her hair. ''Brat.''

Grace had to laugh. Though she'd only known Nick a short while, he'd already stolen a place in her heart. ''I'd better go.''

''Going is good.'' Nick nodded as if she'd said something profound. ''While we're out we can stop and get some ice cream.''

''Ice cream?'' Grace pictured the snow dusting the ground. ''It's twenty degrees outside.''

''But it's warm in the car,'' he said. ''And it'll be warm in the ice cream shop.''

''We didn't eat our dinner,'' Grace said.

"If you don't tell Mrs. Prescott, I won't."

"You're serious about the ice cream."

"Of course I am." Nick winked at her. "I'm always serious when it comes to Rocky Road."

Later, sitting across from him, watching him eat a second bowl of his favorite flavor, Grace was forced to conclude, Nick was indeed serious about his ice cream.

"I've never known anyone to put chocolate syrup on Rocky Road," Grace said, working on her dish of vanilla.

"All I can say is you must have led a very sheltered life," Nick said, wiping some extra chocolate from his lips.

"Sheltered?" Grace thought for a moment, then shook her head. "More like boring."

Though she laughed like she was joking, the words were more true than she cared to admit.

"Why?" Nick put down his spoon and transferred his attention from the Rocky Road to Grace.

Grace shifted uncomfortably under his scrutiny. "What do you mean, why?"

"I mean, why is your life boring?"

Grace started to give him a pat answer, but stopped before the words left her mouth. Why not be honest?

"I'm not much of a risk taker." Grace paused and thought for a moment. "I analyze things to death."

"That's easy to change." He tossed the napkin on the table and stood. "We'll start now."

She put her spoon down and took his outstretched hand. "What do you have in mind?"

"Ice-skating," he said.

Though she'd always wanted to try ice-skating, Grace glanced down at her wool pants and sweater. "I'm not really dressed for…"

"Neither of us is." Nick waved a dismissive hand. "Who cares?"

Grace could make a list a mile long why now wasn't the time to go ice-skating, but Nick might be right. Maybe a little change wouldn't hurt. "Okay, but you'll have to promise to catch me if I fall."

Pulling Grace into his arms every time she became unsteady was a pleasure. Especially after he'd gotten her to say, "Thank you, kind sir," and give him a kiss every time it happened.

At first, she was kissing him almost every other minute, but then she got the hang of skating.

After fifteen minutes without a single fall, Nick was almost ready to trip her himself. He liked the feel of her arms around his neck and the breathless giggles against his face. But what he liked most was just being with her.

Grace was the real thing. There wasn't an ounce of phoniness in her. Even if she'd wanted to lie, she wouldn't be able to pull it off. Her face was way too expressive.

Though she often tried to pretend she didn't care about him, he knew she did. He could see it in her eyes. Along with the fear.

Nick didn't know why she was afraid to care. After all, he hadn't planned on a new relationship, either. He thought he'd go with her for Thanksgiving, and that would be it. But that was before he'd gotten to know her. And though she might be prepared to walk out of his life, he wasn't prepared to let her go.

"Look at me." Grace skated several feet ahead before spinning around with her arms outstretched. "Ta-dah."

Nick smiled. "You're a natural."

Her green eyes sparkled and he could tell his words had pleased her. "Do you really think so?"

He nodded. "In fact you've gotten too good."

She lifted a quizzical brow.

Nick glanced at his watch. "It's been at least a half hour since you've fallen."

As if on cue, her arms began to flail and she called out for help.

He was at her side in an instant, but they were both laughing so hard they lost their balance. They tumbled to the ice in each other's arms.

This time she didn't kiss him on the cheek, but on the mouth.

And by the time they finally got up, Grace wasn't the only one a little shaky on her feet.

Chapter Six

Grace rested the leather-bound menu against the linen tablecloth and pretended to study the wine list. She still wasn't sure why Nick had asked her out tonight. They'd already been to a medical society function with Nellie and Paul on Saturday and they'd gone out for coffee after she'd gotten off work Monday.

When he'd asked her to join him for dinner Friday, she'd almost asked him why. But then she'd decided not to bother. They'd been dating for almost a month and every time she brought up the idea of ending the relationship, he'd change the subject or mention Nellie's continued need for physical therapy.

Grace had to smile. Nick had to know as well as she did that Nellie was deliberately prolonging her time in St. Louis in order to spend time with Paul.

"May I get you something to drink while you wait?" The waiter had already stopped by once since

Nick had left her to say hello to a colleague he'd spotted across the dining room.

"No, thank you." Grace smiled up at the man and realized with a start that she knew him. His hair was a little darker and shorter than when she'd last seen him, and his face was now more of a man's face than a boy's, but it was him. "Jeremy?"

He stared at her for a long moment then his gaze cleared and recognition filled his brown eyes. "Grace?"

"It's been forever." She quickly calculated the time in her head. It had to have been at least five years. Jeremy had volunteered at the clinic the summer before he'd left to attend medical school in California.

"You look fabulous." His gaze lingered and she knew he had to be remembering the days when she'd had flyaway red hair and conservative clothes.

Grace knew she bore little resemblance to her former self. In fact, her appearance had changed drastically just recently.

Last week Nellie had treated her to an afternoon at a day spa. After five hours of having her body waxed, her hair highlighted and trimmed and some lessons in covering up her freckles and enhancing her eyes, even Grace had been impressed at the results. Nellie had been so pleased that she'd promptly booked a session for herself.

When he'd first seen her, Nick had just smiled and said he couldn't imagine that she could have looked any more beautiful, but she did.

Grace once again experienced the flush of pleasure that she'd felt at his words.

"Are you still at the free clinic?"

Jeremy's words pulled Grace back to the present. "Still there. What about you? Are you out of school yet?"

"Graduated from UCLA last year," Jeremy said, a note of pride in his voice. "I'm in a surgical residency program now."

"Congratulations." Grace paused and chose her words carefully. "I know it's none of my business, but if you're a doctor, why are you working here?"

Although Antoine's was one of the nicest restaurants in St. Louis and the tips had to be good, it couldn't begin to compare to what Jeremy could make moonlighting in an emergency room.

Jeremy laughed. "My uncle owns the place. A couple of his servers called in sick. I'd worked here during college so—"

"You decided to help out." It made sense now. Jeremy had been a tireless worker with great compassion for the clinic's clientele. Apparently that same compassion extended to family members in a bind. "That was nice of you."

"It's no big deal," Jeremy said with a dismissive wave. "I kind of enjoy it. Besides, if I hadn't been working tonight, I wouldn't have gotten to see you again."

His gaze dropped to her left hand. "You're not married."

"No, I'm not," Grace said, surprised the admission didn't bother her. "How about you?"

Jeremy laughed again, showing a mouthful of perfect white teeth. "Are you kidding? I've barely had time to breathe these last four years."

Grace laughed with him. There was something warm and genuine about Jeremy.

"Maybe we can get together sometime," Jeremy said. "Catch up."

"I'd like that," Grace said immediately. She'd often wondered what happened to the students after they'd left the clinic.

"Great." Jeremy smiled and leaned over the table, scratching his number on a scrap of paper. "Here's my number—"

Jeremy stopped midsentence and Grace looked up to find that Nick had returned.

"Nick. I didn't see you come back."

"I know," Nick said with an enigmatic smile. "You were...occupied."

His gaze shifted to Jeremy.

"Dr. Tucci." Jeremy straightened.

"Have we met?" Nick's brow furrowed slightly but his tone was pleasant.

"In a roundabout way," Jeremy said, shifting from one foot to the other, his easy smile now strained. "I'm a surgical resident and I've been working with Dr. Brenner. We ran into you in the hall at Children's last week. You also spoke at a seminar I attended."

Grace's gaze shifted from Nick to Jeremy. "I can't believe you two know each other."

"We don't know each other," Jeremy said quickly. "Not really."

"St. Louis isn't that big," Nick said with a shrug. "The medical community tends to be fairly tight."

"I can't believe you're an instructor," Grace teased, thinking of her college professors and knowing none of them had been as handsome as Nick. "What else don't I know?"

Nick pulled out his chair and took a seat. Grabbing her hand he pulled it to his lips and placed a light kiss in the center of her palm then closed her fingers around it. "Sweetheart, you know everything that's important."

Grace could feel her face warm. She wondered if Nick realized the impression he was giving Jeremy.

"Can I get you two some wine?" Jeremy asked, suddenly all business.

Nick shifted his gaze to Grace and raised a brow.

"I prefer white but whatever you like is fine," Grace said.

"Bring us a bottle of—" Nick picked up the folder and quickly scanned the wine list before picking one. Though Grace was by no means a connoisseur, she immediately recognized the dry white vintage. She'd had it only one time, at a wine-tasting class she'd taken at a local community college. It had been her favorite, but far too pricey for her to afford.

Grace shuddered to think what a whole bottle would cost. A house zinfandel would be more than adequate. She opened her mouth to tell Nick when his hand closed over hers and he gave it a squeeze.

Grace closed her mouth without speaking. She needed to remember that Nick had more money than she did and what seemed expensive to her was mere pocket change to him.

"Would you like to order now?" Jeremy asked, his pen poised above the order pad.

"I'm sorry." Grace picked up the menu. "I haven't even—"

"We'll need a little more time," Nick said.

"No problem." Jeremy pocketed the order pad. "I'll be right back with your wine."

The minute Jeremy was out of earshot, Grace turned to Nick. "I can't believe you and Jeremy know each other."

"I was just thinking the very same thing."

"Jeremy used to work at the clinic," Grace said. "He was a very hard worker."

"Were you and he ever—" Nick paused for a long moment "—involved?"

"With Jeremy?" Grace laughed. "He's a boy."

"He's a man, not a boy." Nick took a drink of water and studied her thoughtfully over the top of the glass. "And he's not that much younger than you."

"Well, I still think of him as a boy," Grace said, wondering why Nick had taken a sudden interest in the waiter. "What does it matter anyway? I'm not interested in dating the guy."

"You're right. I don't want to talk about him anyway." Nick's gaze lingered on Grace's lips. "I want to talk about how beautiful you look tonight."

For the first time in her life Grace didn't argue. Tonight she felt beautiful. The black dress she'd chosen was simple yet elegant. The cut flattered her willowy figure and the scoop neckline showed a discreet amount of cleavage. Aunt Nellie had loaned her a strand of pearls. Though she couldn't hold a candle to any of Nick's previous girlfriends, Grace knew she looked good. Not gorgeous by any means, but classically elegant.

"I'm not beautiful," she protested halfheartedly.

He met her gaze. "You are to me."

Butterflies fluttered in her stomach and when Jeremy returned to take their order, Grace barely noticed. In fact, all through dinner, the only thing she was conscious of was Nick: his look, his touch, his laugh. Even the elegant ambiance of the restaurant faded into the background.

On the drive home Grace realized she could get used to having Nick around.

"Penny for your thoughts," he said, casting a sideways glance.

Grace was glad the dim light of the car's interior hid her guilty flush. She wondered what he'd say if she blurted out the truth and told him she was in danger of falling in love with him. She could picture it now; his eyes would turn wary and that easy smile would freeze on his lips. Because he was a nice guy, he'd say something about really caring for her, too. Then he'd change the subject.

"Grace?"

With a start, Grace realized Nick was waiting for an answer. If she was Holly, she'd toss off a one-liner that would make him laugh. But she'd realized long ago that she wasn't witty and charming like her sister, nor was she a sophisticated beauty like the other women Nick had dated.

"I was just thinking what a good time I've had this evening." Even as the words slipped past her lips, Grace knew she was probably breaking some unwritten rule of dating by making such an admission. But then again, she and Nick weren't dating, not really.

He smiled and his shoulders relaxed. For one crazy second Grace had the feeling he'd been worried about her response.

"I had a very nice time, too," he said, pulling into her driveway and turning off the ignition. "In fact, I hate to see the evening end."

"It did go fast," Grace conceded, wishing that they'd lingered longer over dessert.

Nick turned in his seat and took her hand. "How about you invite me in for a drink?"

His thumb massaged Grace's palm. The sensuous touch sent little shivers of electricity up her arm and threatened to short-circuit her good sense. Feeling the way she did about him and knowing they would be all alone, it would be the height of foolishness to let him inside.

Grace took a deep steadying breath. "I don't think that would be a good idea."

For a long moment he sat there, his gaze fixed on her.

Her heart picked up speed and the air was heavy with longing. Grace held her breath. The sensible part of her wanted him to just say good night, but another part hoped he could convince her to let him come inside, at least for a few minutes.

Nick leaned closer and his hand softly cupped her face. "I know you're scared—" he barely whispered the words "—but don't you know I would never hurt you?"

She couldn't help herself. Grace turned her head to his hand and kissed it, her heart aching in her chest.

Because though Nick might not realize it, he'd already broken that promise. The moment he'd flashed her that first smile, he'd sealed her fate.

Nick stared into Grace's eyes. He could see the fear in the emerald depths and hot anger rose inside him. How any man could hurt such a wonderful woman was beyond his comprehension. But she had been hurt, and badly. Her inability to trust told him that.

He longed to tell her that she would never be sorry she'd met him, but he knew words were pointless. He would have to *show* her he could be trusted. And there was no better time to start than now.

"Invite me in," he repeated, offering her a reassuring smile.

He'd been wrong to move so fast in her bedroom

that night. If she let him in her house tonight, he would be on his best behavior. He wouldn't even try to steal as much as a single kiss.

His gaze lowered to her soft sweet lips and Nick quickly amended his hasty promise. Maybe he would give her a good-night kiss or two—but that would be all.

"Nick, I—" Indecision warred on her beautiful features.

"If you'd rather I not, I completely understand." The words were out of his mouth before he had the chance to think them through. But hastily thought out or not, they came from the heart. He would do whatever it took to make Grace happy.

Relief filled her eyes and he was already shrugging aside his disappointment when her hand lightly touched his arm. "I don't have any alcohol, but how about a cup of cocoa?"

His heart picked up speed. At this point he would have agreed to prune juice if it meant he could stay longer. "With marshmallows?"

Her smile widened. "I think that can be arranged."

In only a matter of minutes Nick sat on the sofa in front of a roaring fire with Grace beside him and a steaming cup of cocoa topped with marshmallows in his hand.

Nick heaved a contented sigh. It didn't get much better than this.

His gaze strayed to Grace's mouth. Her last sip of

cocoa had left a thin film of sticky marshmallow on her top lip.

He'd promised himself that he wouldn't kiss her until he was walking out the door. But the urge to taste the tantalizing sweetness tugged at his resolve.

Placing his drink on the end table, Nick turned to Grace. "I've had the best evening."

"Me, too." Grace's tongue swept her lips, removing most of the marshmallow residue, and Nick groaned with frustration.

Grace's brows pulled together and worry filled her gaze. "Are you okay?"

"I will be." He lowered his mouth to hers. The marshmallows were gone but her lips still tasted sweet. And one taste was not enough. Not for Nick. And not for Grace, either, judging by her response. She kissed him back, her mouth pressed eagerly against his.

They sat on the overstuffed cushions and kissed until the hot cocoa grew cold and the fire in the hearth was reduced to glowing embers.

Though Nick could have kissed her forever, the feelings stirring inside him warned that he'd better leave. He didn't want to let things get out of hand. Not when she was beginning to trust him.

"I need to go." Nick released his hold on her and sat back.

Grace fought a surge of disappointment. As much she knew it was a good idea for him to leave before things intensified even more, Grace hated to see the evening end. The whole night had been filled with a certain magic.

And it wasn't just kissing Nick that generated the magic. She'd enjoyed the intimate dinner and conversation immensely. It was amazing how much they had in common.

They both wanted three children and believed that a mother's place was in the home. Though many of Grace's friends were working moms and wouldn't have it any other way, Grace had always dreamed of staying home with her children.

She'd been surprised to find Nick shared her traditional beliefs. Though they'd spoken of their future dreams in only the most general of terms, for a moment Grace had found herself picturing what *their* children would look like—a little boy with her green eyes or a little girl with Nick's dark hair.

She'd visualized herself living in Hazelwood, taking care of the children and making a house a home. She would have time to participate in church activities and put the skills she'd acquired in her gourmet cooking class to good use. But the evenings would be *their* time. When Nick came home she'd be waiting. And late at night, nestled in her husband's arms she'd thank God for sending her the man of her dreams.

"It's late. I'd better get going." Nick stood abruptly. "Tomorrow will come all too soon."

"Will I see you tomorrow?" Grace reluctantly stood, and the words slipped past her lips before she had a chance to stop them.

Nick shook his head and regret laced his handsome features. "I have an event at the country club. Melanie, an old friend of mine, is in charge of a fund-raiser to benefit the music program at one of the local high schools. She asked me months ago to be her escort. Plus Sara is performing."

The lovely fantasy that Grace had spun only moments before shattered into a thousand pieces. Her smile froze on her face.

"It would have been fun to meet your sister-in-law," Grace said, pleased she could sound so off-hand. "She's Sara Michaels, right? The Christian singer?"

"That's right," Nick said. "She's married to my brother Sal. He'll be there, too. In fact the whole family will be out in force."

And your old girlfriend will be on your arm.

Grace had seen Melanie's picture in the society column several times and though she couldn't visualize exactly what Melanie looked like, three words stuck in her mind: *tall, blond* and *gorgeous.* Melanie and Nick were perfect together.

Grace's heart sank. How could she have thought for even one minute that she could compete with such a woman? Her father was a farmer. She worked at a free clinic for the indigent. She'd never fit in with the country club crowd.

It was time she took charge of the situation and broke it off now. But the words died on her lips when Nick pulled her into his arms and murmured how much he was going to miss her.

A tight band gripped Grace's heart, and when Nick kissed her she had to close her eyes against the sudden tears. She returned his kiss with extra fervor, hating herself for being so weak.

How had she ever let herself fall in love with Nick Tucci?

Chapter Seven

"I'm so glad you invited me over this evening," Nellie said, handing Grace her coat. "It seems like forever since we've spent any time together."

Grace hung her aunt's coat in the hall closet and shut the door. "I'm just glad you were free. I thought you and Paul might be going to that fund-raiser at the country club."

Grace hoped Nellie wouldn't pick up the tension in her voice but her aunt just smiled and followed Grace into the living room.

"We were planning to, but a friend of Paul's from medical school called and said he'd be in town and wanted to get together. Paul was going to turn him down, but I told him there would be lots of other events we could attend together."

Grace thought about reminding her aunt that she'd be going back to Iowa in a few weeks, but she kept silent. She wanted this to be a relaxing evening and arguing with Nellie wasn't the way to make that happen.

"Nicholas looked so handsome in his tuxedo." Nellie took a seat on the sofa. "Why didn't you go with him?"

Grace took a seat in the chair. "Nick is escorting his old girlfriend. I imagine after tonight they'll be back together and I won't be seeing him anymore."

Though the words visibly surprised her aunt, they surprised Grace even more. She'd never intended to voice her deepest fears.

"Oh, Gracie." Nellie's eyes filled with concern. "I don't know why he's with another woman tonight, but I do know you don't need to worry. Nicholas loves you."

Her aunt said the words with such conviction that Grace couldn't stop the flare of hope that rose inside her. "Did he tell you that?"

"He didn't have to." Nellie covered Grace's hand with her own. "I can see it in his eyes, the way he looks at you."

Nellie continued to talk, but Grace tuned her out. After all, her aunt's words were merely the ramblings of an incurable romantic, one who lived in a fantasy world where men were honorable and happily-ever-after was part of the picture.

"…I'm going to stay."

The unexpected words jolted Grace back to reality. "Stay?"

"Yes, my dear." Nellie smiled. "I'm staying in St. Louis."

Grace widened her gaze. "But you have to go back."

Nellie laughed as if Grace had said something terribly witty, instead of something that made complete sense.

"What about the library?" Grace asked. "You're just going to walk away from that?"

"I think it will get along quite nicely without me," Nellie said with a wry smile. "Anyway, Mable Applebee has wanted to be head librarian for years."

"But what about my mom?" Grace asked, a tinge of desperation in her tone. Her aunt had always been one of the most sensible women Grace knew. For her to make such a rash decision was totally out of character. "You two are best friends."

"Margaret and I will always be close," Nellie said, "but she's as excited about the changes in my life as I am."

"Mom thinks it's a good idea for you to stay in St. Louis?" Grace said slowly, skepticism evident in her tone.

Nellie's smile widened. "Margaret knows a bride needs to be with her husband."

"Bride?" Grace shook her head as if that would clear the confusion. "What are you talking about?"

"Paul and I are getting married."

Nellie's tone was matter-of-fact but Grace noticed her aunt's flushed cheeks and the sparkle in her eyes.

"You're engaged?"

"It's official." Nellie held out her left hand and

for the first time Grace saw the large marquis-cut diamond.

At the sight of the huge stone, Grace's mouth dropped open. She snapped it shut. She'd had no idea Nellie and Paul were so serious.

"We're getting married on the twenty-fourth."

"Christmas Eve?" Grace's words came out as a high-pitched squeak. "That's next Thursday."

"It was Paul's idea. He says all he wants for Christmas is me." Nellie's blush deepened.

Grace sat back in the chair. She couldn't believe it. Her aunt—her maiden aunt—was going to marry a man she'd just met. Since Grace's own mother had apparently given her blessing, that left Grace to be the voice of reason. Men could be cruel and the last thing she wanted was to see her aunt hurt. "But you barely know the guy. Aunt Nellie, you have to be sensible."

"I don't need to be anything but happy," Nellie said firmly, meeting Grace's gaze. "I love Paul. And he loves me."

Grace stifled a groan. Her aunt was even more of a romantic than she'd thought. "But you two just met."

"You know when it's right." Her aunt lifted her chin in a stubborn gesture. "Take you and Nicholas for example. Can you honestly tell me that you didn't know right off the bat that he was the one for you?"

The tantalizing option of lying hung before Grace, but Nellie had been honest and Grace owed her the same courtesy.

"I knew I loved him within days," Grace said reluctantly. "What I've never been sure of is how he feels about me."

The words were out in the open now, like cards lying face-up on the table.

Nellie stared at her for a long moment. "Have you told Nicholas you love him?"

Grace shook her head. She hadn't been able to control her heart but thankfully she had been able to keep her mouth shut. That way, when he dumped her, she would at least have her pride.

"You're afraid, aren't you?" Compassion and love filled Nellie's gaze. "Afraid he doesn't love you back?"

Something inside Grace exploded. "Of course I'm afraid. Look at me. Look at him. He could have any woman he wants. I'd be stupid to think he'd ever pick *me*."

Tears welled up in her eyes but Grace refused to cry. Still, when her aunt opened her purse and pulled out a tissue, Grace took it.

Grace expected her aunt to at least offer a token protest, maybe tell her she was being foolish, that she was perfect for him and he did love her. But Nellie did none of these things. Instead her aunt's gaze turned sharp and assessing.

"Tell me about Nicholas," Nellie said abruptly. "Tell me what you like about him."

Grace didn't know where Nellie was going with this, but she decided to humor her aunt.

"Nick is a genuinely nice guy," Grace began. "He doesn't judge people, he…"

Once Grace started talking, she couldn't seem to stop. She told Nellie about the fun the two of them had together, the way he made her laugh when she was blue, the common values and faith they shared.

After Grace finished, there wasn't a shred of doubt in either woman's mind about the depth of Grace's feelings.

"Nicholas sounds like a wonderful man," Nellie said.

"He certainly is." Grace heaved a heavy sigh.

"Do you realize," Nellie said, "that when you were listing his virtues, you never once mentioned how handsome he is?"

"That's because it goes without saying," Grace said.

"Gracie, I'm trying to make a point and you're not helping."

Nellie's indignant tone made Grace smile. "I'm sorry. What's your point?"

"That you don't love Nicholas for his *looks*, but for who he *is*." Nellie pointed her finger at Grace for extra emphasis.

"I see what you're saying," Grace said. "That it's the internal stuff that counts. And I agree. But it's one-sided. Men love beautiful women."

"Are you saying Nicholas is shallow?" Nellie lifted a brow, surprise evident in her tone.

"All men are shallow, Aunt Nellie," Grace said finally. "And Nick is a man. You do the math."

*　*　*

All men are shallow.

Grace shut her eyes and willed herself to go to sleep. She'd already tried counting sheep and progressive relaxation. But though she was exhausted, sleep eluded her. She kept thinking of what she'd told her aunt.

Though she hadn't wanted to make Nick look bad by saying he was shallow, she also hadn't wanted to admit her real fear—that Nick just didn't want *her*. That maybe it wasn't her appearance at all. That maybe she just wasn't smart enough, or interesting enough, to keep Nick's attention.

She was scared to admit how much she cared, because she couldn't take it if he didn't feel the same. And now she had the added fear that he was getting back together with his old girlfriend.

She forced the thought from her mind and reminded herself that whatever happened would be God's will.

Grace rested her head on the pillow and closed her eyes. *Dear God. Please let me accept the fact that You know what's best for me. That You have a plan for my life. That—*

Grace stiffened and the prayer died on her lips. Was someone at her door?

She held her breath and listened. A light tapping sound echoed through the silent rooms and icy fingers of fear traveled up her spine.

Her apartment was on the second floor and the stairway was open to the outside. Anyone could be out there. For the first time since she'd moved in, Grace wished she lived in a secured building.

She shifted her gaze to the phone. She could call the police, but what would she say? Someone's knocking at my front door?

Grabbing her robe from the end of the bed, Grace wrapped it tightly around her and moved quietly to the living room. The apartment might not have a security system, but thankfully her door did have a dead bolt and a peephole.

Grace held her breath and peered through the hole. When she saw who it was, the breath she'd been holding came out in a whoosh. Flipping the dead bolt, Grace pulled open the door. "Nick. What are you doing here?"

He smiled. "I thought I'd stop by and say hello."

Grace glanced at the clock on the wall. "It's two-thirty in the morning."

His smile never faltered. "Does that mean I can't come in?"

Grace hesitated only a second. She waved him in and shut the door against the cold.

He'd barely gotten inside before he turned toward her. Suddenly the large living room seemed too small.

Nellie was right. He did look fantastic in his tux. His broad shoulders filled out the dark jacket and fit him so perfectly it almost looked hand-tailored. And to top it off, he smelled wonderful. His cologne was a popular men's fragrance and one of her favorites.

Though the hardwood floor was cold against her

bare feet and a cool chill hung in the air, a delicious warmth filled Grace. She cleared her throat and forced a nonchalant air.

"Would you like something to drink?" she asked, walking toward the kitchen.

Nick shook his head. "I'm fine. Anyway, I didn't come over for that."

"Then why did you come?" Grace stopped and took a seat in the room's only chair, leaving him no choice but to sit on the sofa.

"Because I missed you," he repeated with a rueful grin. "I know it sounds corny, but all night all I could think of was you."

"Sounds like your little reunion with Melanie didn't go well." Grace crossed her legs. If he thought he could spend all evening with his old girlfriend and then come over and she'd fall into his arms, he was mistaken.

"Melanie was fine," Nick said with a dismissive wave. "Other than she had some crazy idea we were getting back together."

"Hmm." Grace lifted a finger to her lips. "I wonder what could have given her that idea? Maybe because you were her date for such an important function—"

"I told you, she asked *me*," Nick interrupted.

"And you said yes," Grace pointed out. "Knowing how much she likes you, you still said yes."

"I was doing her a favor."

Grace gave an unladylike snort. "She's a beautiful

woman. She could have easily found another escort.''

Nick raked a hand through his hair. ''You don't understand.''

Grace stood and walked to the door. Beneath her robe her legs were trembling, but when she spoke her voice was calm. She was not going to let herself get hurt again. ''You're right. I don't understand. You take your old girlfriend to one of the biggest parties of the year, then you come over here in the middle of the night and expect me to fall all over you. I can tell you one thing. It ain't gonna happen.''

''What's going on?'' Nick's lips tightened. ''You said you understood about tonight.''

Grace's hand rested on the doorknob. ''I thought I did, but your coming over here tonight made me realize I had it all wrong.''

Nick stood and stared, not saying a word.

''You don't care about me,'' Grace said matter-of-factly, the words tearing at her heart. ''If you did, you would have taken me tonight. I would have been the one at your side. I would have been the one meeting your family and friends. But no, I'm only good enough for some after-hours kissing.''

''Grace.'' Nick crossed the room in several strides. But when he reached for her, Grace stepped back and opened the door.

''Goodbye, Nick.'' Grace met his disbelieving gaze head-on. ''It's been great knowing you.''

She fully expected him to leave, maybe muttering

some brief platitudes on his way out. But his jaw set in a stubborn line and he didn't budge an inch.

"I'll go now, if that's what you want," he said finally. "But we need to talk. I'll pick you up tomorrow at six and we'll have dinner at the Grotto."

"What if I'm not here?"

"I spent a long weekend in Iowa," he said. "I'm only asking for one evening."

He held her gaze for a moment then turned on his heel and left.

Grace stared after Nick, then lifted her gaze heavenward.

Dear God, what do I do now?

Chapter Eight

The garage door rumbled to a close behind the Land Rover. Nick turned off the engine, muttering a curse when the key caught momentarily in the ignition. All the way home his anger had been mounting.

He'd always heard that redheads had a temper, but he'd never seen that side of Grace until tonight.

The evening had gone bad from the start. He'd endured Melanie's clinging and inane conversation with one thought in mind—seeing Grace at evening's end.

When he'd dropped Melanie off, he hadn't even been conscious of the time. Looking back, 2:00 a.m. may have been a bit late to stop over but still, her tirade had been out of line. He thought she'd be happy to see him, no matter what the time.

Nick wiped a weary hand across his face. It was unbelievable how something so good could go bad so quickly.

Entering the house a few minutes later, he tried to walk softly. Eleanora was a light sleeper and he wasn't in the mood to talk.

When he saw the light coming from the living room, Nick groaned. His bad luck had followed him home.

Heaving a resigned sigh, Nick entered the room. "Eleanora, I can't believe you're still up."

Nellie lifted her gaze from the romance novel she was reading and placed the book in her lap.

"She sent you home." Nellie's voice rang with satisfaction.

Nick stared. "What are you talking about?"

"Gracie." Nellie shifted her gaze to the mantle clock. "You were with her."

"I stopped by her house," Nick said, feeling as if he were sixteen again and had missed a curfew. He plopped into a nearby chair and exhaled a weary sigh. "And you're right. She told me to leave."

"Good for her," Nellie said. "I don't care if she loves you or not. It's not proper for a single woman to entertain a gentleman friend in her apartment—"

"Whoa, wait one minute." Nick straightened in the chair and wondered if his foggy brain was playing tricks on him. "Say that again."

Nellie paused and blinked several times, clearly nonplussed at being interrupted. "You know it's not proper—"

"No, not that." Though his mother would cringe at his poor manners, Nick stopped her. "The one before that. About her loving me."

Nellie's brow rose. "I said her loving you doesn't—"

"How do you know she loves me?" Nick demanded, not caring if he was interrupting her again.

"She told me so," Nellie said matter-of-factly.

Happiness bubbled up inside him. Obviously her holding back hadn't meant she didn't care. *She loves me.* The night that had seemed so dark only moments before, now was bright. He leaned back in his chair and laughed, suddenly lighthearted.

Nellie's gaze narrowed. "Nicholas, have you been drinking?"

Nick's smile widened. "A couple of glasses of wine with dinner. Why do you ask?"

"Because you're acting strange," Nellie said.

"Strange?" Nick chuckled, wondering what Eleanora would do if he suddenly burst into song. He chuckled again. "I'm just happy."

Now that he knew Grace loved him, all was right with the world. Tonight's episode fell into perspective. She'd been hurt and jealous, and it was all his fault.

He'd never told her he loved her. He'd never even taken the time to introduce her to his family.

Nick would remedy both those oversights tomorrow night. Grace would meet his family. Later, when they were alone, he'd confess his love. Then he'd ask her to marry him.

It was a good solid plan, practically foolproof. After all, she loved him and he loved her. What could go wrong?

* * *

Grace glanced at the clock and hurriedly finished fixing her hair. After the way she'd acted last night, she wanted to at least be ready when Nick arrived.

Shame rose up inside her. She'd behaved like such a shrew. Granted he shouldn't have come knocking at her door in the middle of the night, but she could have handled the situation with a little more maturity. After all, she had no claim on him.

And she'd practically shut the door in his face. All because she'd been jealous.

Grace heaved a resigned sigh. She'd really blown it. Hadn't she learned long ago that men didn't put up with such theatrics? They didn't have to be understanding, because there were plenty of women who would give them their space and smile while doing it.

As sure as she knew her own name, she knew that tonight over a dessert and coffee, Nick would end the relationship. Though it didn't make sense to her why he hadn't done it when she'd practically ordered him out of the house, she'd finally concluded he had too much class to end even a brief relationship in such an uncivilized manner.

She turned away from the mirror and blinked back unexpected tears. Though she'd told herself since day one that this relationship would be short-lived and had mentally prepared herself, the knowledge didn't lessen the pain she now felt.

In some ways she wished she could just call him and break it off. Her gaze drifted longingly toward the phone. It would be a coward's way out, but it would be better than trying to keep it together at a restaurant.

Last night, she'd been angry and in control. Now all she felt was sad.

Grace's hand inched closer to the phone and her heart picked up speed. Her fingers closed around the receiver. But she couldn't bring herself to pick it up. Because Aunt Nellie wasn't the only romantic in the family. And though Grace was ninety-nine percent sure tonight would be the end, a tiny spark of hope still flickered.

Maybe he doesn't want to break up with me. Maybe he wants to tell me he loves me.

The thought had been tugging at her all day. Though she knew it was crazy, she'd still dressed with extra care—selecting a green jersey dress that hugged her curves and accentuated her eyes. She'd even taken extra time with her hair, blow drying it straight so that it lay softly against her shoulders. And the new shade of lipstick that she'd bought over lunch made her lips look full and kissable.

She could feel his fingers weaving through her hair as his lips closed over—

The telephone rang and Grace jumped back, pulling the receiver from its base and knocking it to the floor.

Her heart pounding, Grace snatched the phone from the floor. "Hello."

"Oh, hello." A feminine voice paused. "May I speak with Grace Comstock, please?"

"This is Grace Comstock."

"Ms. Comstock, I'm calling from Children's Hospital for Dr. Nicholas Tucci. He—"

"Before you go any further I need to tell you that Nick isn't here," Grace said. "But I am expecting him anytime, so I can have him call, or you could try his pager...."

"Ma'am, I'm aware Dr. Tucci isn't there." A hint of amusement sounded in the woman's voice. "That's why I'm calling. He's been unexpectedly delayed in surgery and wanted to know if he could meet you at the restaurant."

Grace paused, wondering if this could be her out. But as quickly as the thought entered her mind, she discarded it. "That would be fine. What time?"

"Dr. Tucci indicated he should be able to make it by seven."

"I'll be there."

"Have a good evening," the secretary said.

"You, too," Grace said, and hung up the phone.

She glanced at the clock. An hour's reprieve. At this point she didn't know whether to be upset...or relieved.

Sal Tucci stood next to the wall of the Grotto and wondered if this occasion really warranted wearing a tie.

He glanced around the crowded lobby noting casually dressed men. But when Sara had heard the purpose of tonight's hastily arranged family dinner, she'd insisted on the tie, as well as the sport coat and dress slacks.

Sal ran his finger around the inside of his collar. His younger brother had dated lots of women over the years, but none of them had ever come close to capturing his heart. But this one had. Sal could hear it in Nick's voice. His brother was finally in love. Sal could recognize the symptoms because he had the same affliction.

A moment later, Sal caught a glimpse of his wife exiting the ladies' room. He couldn't help but smile. With her long blond hair and big blue eyes, Sara drew admiring glances wherever she went. But when she caught his eyes and smiled, he felt a surge of pride. She was his. Every day he thanked God for bringing her into his life.

In only moments she stood before him and his arm automatically circled her waist. "Are you feeling better?"

"I'm still a little queasy." Sara laid her hand on her rounded ball of a stomach. "I knew I should have eaten something before I left the house."

She raised a hand to her brow and swayed slightly and Sal tightened his grip.

As a former undercover police officer, Sal had seen his share of hazardous duty and he wasn't ashamed to admit he'd been afraid a time or two. But that was nothing compared to what he felt now, holding his pregnant wife.

"I'll get you something right now," Sal said,

panic edging his tone. He looked around, trying to find a waiter to flag down.

"Honey—" Sara smiled reassuringly "—I'm fine. Really. Once we sit down, we'll order an appetizer and—"

"Is this the reason you invited me here?" The feminine voice was filled with anger. "To humiliate me?"

Sal jerked his head up at the sound of the angry voice. A young woman stood before him, her hands on her hips.

"You cad." With a strength that would have done a longshoreman proud, the woman slapped Sal across the face.

Even as Sal took the blow he stepped protectively in front of Sara. But the woman had already turned on her heel and headed toward the door.

You could have heard a pin drop. Sal forced a laugh, his hand rising to rub his stinging cheek.

"Mistaken identity," he told the onlookers.

"What was that about?" Sara's eyes were wide and her voice trembled.

Sal pulled his wife close in a comforting embrace while his gaze shifted to the doorway just in time to see the woman leave.

"Red hair. Green eyes. Great figure." Sal smiled, still rubbing his cheek. "I think I just met the woman Nick is going to marry."

Chapter Nine

Grace wrapped her arms around herself and headed down the sidewalk. Though it was warm for December, forty degrees was still too cold to be walking without a coat.

But she'd rather freeze to death on the streets of St. Louis than go back in that restaurant and face Nick and Melanie. How could he have brought her? And for what purpose? To tell Grace what she already knew—that she couldn't hold a candle to the gorgeous socialite?

Melanie was even more beautiful in person than in those old newspaper photographs. Her hair was a silvery blond that fell in loose waves past her shoulders. And her eyes that had been nondescript in the black-and-white photos had been large and startlingly blue.

Though Melanie was striking, Grace hadn't initially noticed her. Grace had been checking her coat when she'd caught a glimpse of Nick standing against the far wall. The waiting area was crowded, and by the time Grace got close, Melanie had reached him.

The look in his eyes when he'd seen the statuesque blonde had taken Grace's breath away. It was obvious the two were lovers.

Grace had decided right then and there that she was just going to walk out the door without saying a word. Until she'd seen the blonde at a different angle and realized that she wasn't just beautiful, she was *pregnant.*

You cad.

The words she'd uttered ran through her mind like a grade B movie.

Cad? Did anyone even use that word anymore?

Grace set her lips in a grim line remembering the shock in Nick's eyes. Whether he was familiar with the word or not, she was sure he'd gotten the message. But if he had the nerve to ever call her again, she'd be glad to let him know in no uncertain terms what she thought of his immoral behavior.

That's why, when the Land Rover pulled into an alley blocking her path and Nick pushed open the door, Grace got in.

"Mind telling me what you're doing walking in this weather without a coat?"

Grace had to give him points for his acting ability. Obviously he had even more talent for deception than she'd realized. And even though the best defense had always been a good offense, Grace wanted to tell him that only worked when both players were in the game. As far as she was concerned, this game was over.

"Mind telling me why you didn't tell me Melanie was pregnant with your baby?" Grace shot back.

"Melanie is pregnant?"

If she hadn't seen the two of them together, the shocked look on his face would have been believable. Instead it was laughable.

"Oh, c'mon, Nick." Grace couldn't keep the disgust from her voice. "I just saw the two of you. It was obvious—"

"Saw us?" Nick's voice was filled with confusion. "Where? What are you talking about?"

"You know very well what I'm talking about." Either Nick was a pathological liar or he thought she was incredibly stupid. Either way, Grace refused to play along. "I suppose you've already forgotten that I slapped you?"

"You slapped someone?"

"I don't know what kind of game you're playing—"

Suddenly Nick started laughing. "I can't believe it. You hit Sal."

Grace frowned, not finding one ounce of humor in this whole situation. "Sal?"

"My older brother." Nick shook his head and chuckled. "He's the one married to Sara Michaels. People say we look a lot alike, except his eyes are hazel and mine are blue."

Grace thought back. She remembered the man's startled gaze, but she couldn't recall his eyes.

A knot formed in the pit of her stomach. "Your sister-in-law's pregnant?"

Nick nodded. "Due in April."

"But why were they at the Grotto?" Grace had a feeling she didn't want to know.

"To meet you." Nick's gaze met hers. "My whole family is there now, waiting for us."

"But why?"

"Because I asked them," Nick said. "I told them I wanted them to meet the woman I was going to marry."

Grace's heart slammed against her rib cage and all she could do was stare.

"I'm serious." Nick put the vehicle into park and shut off the engine. "I love you, Grace. Please say you'll be my wife."

Grace hesitated and thought of her greatest fear— that she'd profess her love and he'd back off, or maybe even laugh at her. But the more she pondered the point, the more she realized that the Nick Tucci she'd come to know and love was an honorable man. He wouldn't say he loved her if he didn't. He wouldn't have brought up marriage if he wasn't serious.

The lump in Grace's stomach now rose and blocked her throat. "You really want to marry me?"

Nick nodded and his gaze softened. "If you'll have me?"

"I slapped your brother."

Nick seemed to find her horrified tone amusing. He smiled and took her hands in his. "Don't worry. He's used to it. When Sal was a cop, people were always punching him."

Grace pulled away from his amused smile and covered her face with her hands. "I can't believe I acted that way."

"Sweetheart, this isn't your fault. It's mine," he said. "I should have told you how I felt long before this. But I didn't want to rush you. But when your aunt told me you loved me—"

"Aunt Nellie said that?" Grace sat up straight. "I told her that in confidence."

"She didn't betray your confidence," Nick said. "She thought I already knew."

"Still, she had no right—"

"She has every right. She loves you and wants you to be happy," Nick said. "I want to be happy, too. And I will be if you'll agree to be my wife."

Grace could scarcely breathe. "Is this a dream?"

"It's no dream." Nick folded her into his arms. "I love you. I want you to be my wife, Grace. If you will, I promise I'll spend the rest of my life making you happy."

She gently touched his cheek. "I love you, Nick."

He smiled and she could see happiness in his eyes, happiness and contentment and a deep inner peace.

"And I will marry you," Grace said softly. "But I do have one condition."

Nick stilled. "What's that?"

Grace flashed an impish smile, unable to stay serious for a moment longer. "That you stand between your brother and I the first time we're introduced."

Nick laughed out loud. "Sweetheart, don't you worry about Sal. He's going to love you. All my family will."

"Your family." Grace sat up straight. "They're waiting at the restaurant. We need to go."

"Not so fast." Nick reached into his pocket and pulled out a tiny velvet box. "First you need to put this on."

Grace slowly opened the lid and stared at a glittering diamond that had to be at least three carats. "It's beautiful."

He carefully lifted the ring out and took her left hand, placing it on her finger. "Forever."

Grace swallowed hard and met his gaze.

"Forever," she said. And as his lips lowered to hers, she found herself hoping what everyone said was true: that forever was indeed a long, long time.

Epilogue

"I could stay here all day." Grace cuddled up next to her husband of three weeks. Between his body heat and the thick down comforter, she was toasty warm.

"Me, too." Nick's eyes took on a wicked gleam and his arm tightened around her.

Though they'd been husband and wife for almost a month, Grace couldn't help but blush. Such intimacy was still new to her. But the simple touch of his fingers against her skin reawakened her desire. Grace turned her face to her husband, eager for his kiss. If she'd known what she'd been missing, she would have eloped instead of waiting almost a year to become Nick's wife.

Just as Nick's mouth closed over hers, Grace caught a glimpse of the time on the bedside clock. Her heart skipped a beat. She jerked upright, ignoring his frustrated moan. "It's eleven o'clock."

"So?" Nick tugged at her arm, his eyes dark with promise.

"We have to be at Paul and Nellie's in less than a half hour and we're not even dressed." Grace swung her legs over the side of the bed and stood.

"We can have turkey and stuffing any old time." Nick patted the empty spot beside him on the bed.

His gaze slid over her body and Grace had to force herself to remember that this was Paul and Nellie's first Thanksgiving as husband and wife.

"We can't disappoint Nellie," Grace said. "She's been working on this dinner all week."

"With your help," Nick pointed out.

"It was a pleasure." Grace smiled, knowing the words were true. Her closeness with her aunt was only one of many things she had to be thankful for this year. She also had a new husband, a new home and—her hand strayed to her stomach—hopefully a new baby on the way.

She and Nick had decided they wanted to start a family right away. And though she hadn't taken a pregnancy test yet, all other signs indicated she'd conceived.

"And, even if we'd skip the dinner, which I'd never do," Grace added, "we can't skip church."

Nick was silent for a long moment. "We *do* have a lot to be thankful for."

"We've been truly blessed," Grace said in a soft voice, grabbing her robe and pulling it on. "Last year at this time I was convinced I'd never have a love of my own."

"I was starting to think the same thing," Nick admitted. "And then I realized that love had been right under my nose all along."

" 'To everything there is a season,' " Grace murmured. The familiar verse had been going through her head all week as she'd reflected on the past year.

If she'd met Nick earlier, he might not have been ready to settle down. If love had come quickly and easily, she might not have appreciated it as much.

Her gaze settled on her husband and her heart warmed. She'd reaped a bountiful harvest, one that, God willing, would bear fruit for years to come. And for that, and so much more, Grace knew she'd spend the rest of her life giving God thanks and praise.

* * * * *

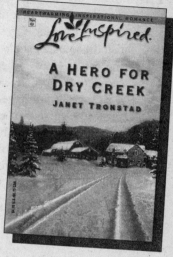

Love Inspired®

SEPTEMBER LOVE

BY

VIRGINIA MYERS

Fiftysomething Beth Colby thought her life was complete—after years of being a single mother and widow, she found a second chance at love, with Doug Colby. But was her new marriage ready for the permanent addition of Doug's rambunctious toddler grandson?

Don't miss

SEPTEMBER LOVE

On sale November 2003

Available at your favorite retail outlet.

A journey of discovery and healing through faith and love.

The
Christmas
Kite

What happens when the magic of the Christmas season touches the lives of a single mother, her eight-year-old Down's syndrome son and a reclusive stranger?

Follow the tale of a kite to find out!

"Gail Gaymer Martin writes with compassion and understanding...."
—*Romantic Times*

Available in November 2003, wherever books are sold!

Steeple
Hill®

Visit us at www.steeplehill.com